Advance Praise for *The Hearing Test*

"In this striking novel, 'controlled panic' gives way to a cool remove when a young artist suddenly goes deaf. Silence, for her, 'is dressed as an injury,' but it is also the point of entry into the lives of other creators, and philosophers. Elegant and startling, *The Hearing Test* is a contemplative gem."

—AMY HEMPEL

"An artist suffering from sudden hearing loss finds herself even more sensitive to the lives of others, observing neighbors and the absurdities of the city, always punctuated by art and literary gossip. This debut work by Eliza Callahan is an extraordinary piece of literature, to be read alongside the novels of W. G. Sebald, Rachel Cusk, and María Gainza."

—KATE ZAMBRENO, author of *Drifts*

"Eerie and tender and utterly consuming, *The Hearing Test* has built an entirely new world from the materials of the one we know. It takes you to a restaurant called the void, *Il Vuoto*, and serves you its primal, beguiling sustenance: a nourishment of pauses, estrangement, and bewilderment. The voice here is wise and wry and wondering; in its fresh and faltering silences are frequencies I've never heard before. From the first paragraph, I knew I wanted to keep reading Eliza Barry Callahan forever."

—LESLIE JAMISON, author of *Splinters* and *The Empathy Exams*

"Not for a while have I read a book by a writer new to me, and felt so much toward it so fast. *The Hearing Test* takes up fragility, sound and silence, solitude, the unknown, and the self in relation to others with a light, yet serious touch. I've found a new favorite."

—AMINA CAIN, author of *Indelicacy*

"A young woman's sudden hearing loss initiates and propels *The Hearing Test*. But affliction is also a catalyst for the many irresistible twists and digressions that make this novel of *dérive* so compelling. Callahan never explains; with steely reserve she observes and chronicles, makes ingenious, delirious connections and transitions, and takes us on a journey through her cultural mindscape of artists, writers, cinema and music, offering it up with muted irony and a limpid grace. *The Hearing Test* is ecstatic prose."   —MOYRA DAVEY, author of *Index Cards*

THE

HEARING

TEST

THE
HEARING
TEST

A NOVEL

ELIZA BARRY CALLAHAN

CATAPULT  NEW YORK

for D and M

I want to know more about likelihood.
I pull the hood over my head.
Things get quieter.

THE
HEARING
TEST

PREFACE

I HAVE A habit, since I can remember, of reading plot summaries of movies and books before watching or reading them. Last July a friend from Russia recommended the 1967 Soviet film *July Rain*. She said something about it was very relevant to me. And when I asked her in what sense she just said the word *generally*. I began the film and was enjoying it but I fell asleep and never went back to finish. I always seem to begin things late at night . . .

But before I watched *July Rain*, I found a translated summary that read:

> The heroes of the film are almost thirty and very often at this time people have a period of revision of the positions already developed earlier. That it is sometimes associated with loss. That

the heroine of this film comes to such revision. And that she has a lot to think about again. That she begins to understand that her previous assessment of the surface all appears to her in a different, more clear and sharp light. That she loses her former closest person who becomes a stranger and distant.

I wrote to my friend to let her know that she was right, that the film was a double, a score of the recent events of my life charted for me in brushstrokes the size of trees.

I found myself stuck on the score. The score as a map or directive, a tally, a musical accompaniment to a moving image. The score as a cut into a surface, and even indebtedness. I thought about it now. How a score could be what leads me or a record of where I've been, or both at once. Not a representation of my reality but rather its analog. How I kept score of a year in which I was flung suddenly from my own life, only to learn that to see something in its entirety is to be entirely outside of that thing. How I took one long walk around myself. How I wrote it down—the stark, inescapable facts of a situation.

On August 29, 2019, I was meant to travel to Venice to watch a lifelong friend get married—a small reception for just ten people. The friend was marrying a Venetian. When I awoke that morning, I felt a deep drone in my right ear accompanied by a sound I can best compare to a large piece of sheet metal being rocked, a perpetually rolling thunder. I moved from the bedroom to the living room in a controlled panic, where my little black dog stood by the door and barked. It was just past time for her morning walk. The bark, the first distinct, external sound I had heard since waking, was distorted and distant.

When I called out her name, I found my own voice sounded unfamiliar. The volume had been dialed up and the pitch had shifted. A few days earlier, I had been swimming in the Rockaways after a heavy summer rain, and I thought maybe the city water had taken hold.

I went immediately to see a doctor—my flight was scheduled for the late afternoon. At the emergency ear-and-eye clinic, a young nurse looked into my ears. No, I told her, I was not in any pain. She said they looked beautiful and clean, which she then added was not a good sign. After a hearing test, the doctor looked over some graphs and then into my eyes and said, Bad luck. This was a diagnosis. I had been struck by Sudden Deafness. The term sounded so severe that it verged on comedic for the wingspan of one moment. He said I had lost low-end hearing. There was an explanation for the loss of sound— something had attacked the nerve between the inner ear and the brain—but there was no explanation for the cause. The rolling thunder, he explained, was a result of the brain attempting to replace the frequencies the ear had lost.

Quickly, I became a person of interest. I was referred to three specialists, researchers in the field, who made specific room in their schedules to see me over the next two days. Fees and copays were waived. Within forty-eight hours, each specialist relayed that I was unlikely to make a full recovery, or any recovery at all—worse, one said, it could mean the onset of a degenerative hearing disease that typically affects people late in life and concludes in a profound deafness. The sincerest strain of quiet.

We can get to the moon, another doctor said, but we can't get to the inner ear. This doctor proposed what he referred to as an "attempt-rescue"—a procedure that had no proven positive or negative outcome. The attempt-rescue would entail a local anesthetic and a small javelin-like instrument that would be used to puncture directly through the drum. After they had created the hole in the drum, a needle would retrace the javelin's path and push steroids somewhere toward the problem area. I agreed to the procedure, which took place the following morning, at the same time as the late-afternoon wedding reception. The bride's mother sent a photo of nine white folding chairs on a patio facing the Adriatic Sea: *The show must go on . . .*

I had just moved into a one-room apartment with my little black dog. My landlord, I learned, was a painter known for figurative works laden with symbolic meaning. A fan of Pierre Bonnard, her subject was primarily herself and the paintings took form as conventional self-portraits and fragmented close-ups—oil on linen. A critic had compared them to the short stories of Chekhov. It seemed this critic was also a personal friend. The landlord had lived in the apartment thirty-five years ago, had used it as a studio for five years, and hadn't set foot inside the place for ten. She had employed a man, a documentary-film editor, to look after it, liaise with the tenants, and collect the rent. She had neither the time nor the energy for leaks, locksmiths, or tired drains . . . The editor, a previous tenant himself, told me that he hoped to one day buy the place, should the painter change her mind and finally decide to sell. When we met in front of the building to sign the necessary documents, he told me that even though I had signed the lease and was moving in the following week, the landlord wanted to interview me, out of curiosity. She had a busy schedule and wouldn't be available until after I moved in.

When we met in the small park two blocks from the apartment two weeks later, the landlord asked me if there was still a fireplace in the one-room apartment, and I found it funny that she was asking me this about her own home. I told her I did not recall a fireplace. Someone must have taken it away or covered it up, she said with heavy suspicion. In the interview, she did not ask me any questions about myself. She did say that her happiest times were spent there in the apartment, before she had children, and noted that it was good that I was small like she was—I would be able to stand up straight in the shower without issue. She suggested doing dishes in the shower, too, which sat behind a bifold door in the kitchen just next to the apartment's only sink. The water pressure is more determined in the shower, she said, and you can get two things done at once.

She told me that the southern light that came in was special because it was muted perfectly by the way the buildings stood at different angles and heights in the back courtyard. Direct-direct light is a real hassle, she said. She said the light in the apartment was very androgynous. The courtyard on which the apartment's two windows looked out was the courtyard from *Rear Window*, she told me. Hitchcock had shot footage from the roof and other surrounding buildings in order to construct his set, a near-perfect replica. It's very funny, she said, when she lived in the apartment the super had actually murdered a tenant. I said the super seemed nice. She said he was new.

She added that the view from our window was the exact view that the invalid has from his window in the film. She said *our* like it was our apartment, like we lived there together. The thing is, she said, our same view is sitting there in Hollywood on Melrose Avenue, somewhere on the Paramount lot, covered in a cape of dust. She said this was fitting because she was someone who always made sure to have two of everything she liked, *just in case*. She told me she had two of the same shirt she was wearing right then. It's as if this block, this courtyard, were a smear of wet ink on paper that had been folded in half—that's how it had gotten to the other side, to California. This country is the real Rorschach test and in the middle, it's just a lot of illegible darkness. You'll see . . . All we can do is read the edges.

She said that our apartment on the Hollywood set actually had plumbing, probably better than ours here. In the snow, I often thought our courtyard was the model for the real thing, she said, not the other way around, and sometimes I wondered if the sun was actually just one thousand lights on a dimmer.

It was early August then and I always left my window open as wide as it could go. I found that in the courtyard, in the very place where the murderer tended to his patch of flowers, under which his wife's head sat in a hatbox, an overweight day trader would often pace in straight lines wearing a headpiece shouting about the rise and fall of numbers as if the numbers, like tides, were tied to the moon.

At the end of the interview the landlord asked what I would do to pay the rent that I was already paying. She asked if I had a guarantor. I said that I was my own guarantor. Over the last year, I had stopped assisting

a mid-career conceptual artist and had fallen by accident into scoring short things: commercials, student
films, whatever came my way. I had enough saved for
a year's rent. Nothing is an accident, she said.

I had made a score for a friend's film set in the
American West about a teenage boy who meets a
young man at a cherry stand passing through his
small town by bike; the boy follows the man to a
cruising site in rural Oregon, they kiss, and the man
leaves. This friend had been aware of my classically
trained childhood. This had led to a score for a commercial for an environmentally friendly lipstick
company, then a score for a film about a girl who
becomes a fish after eating a piece of fish offered to
her by another traveler, an older man from Japan, as
they ride a train to the Bay of Cádiz. There was also
a short film about a girl who tells her boyfriend that
she was assaulted by her boss the night before, after
karaoke, and her boyfriend's inability to feel anything but jealousy. There was a commercial using
just the sounds of trains for a high-quality luggage
manufacturer from Cologne known for lightweight
aluminum suitcases. There was a film about a young
American couple abroad in Valparaíso, Chile, who
can't decide whether or not they're still in love.

I told the landlord that, at first, I'd found it entertaining, and that I welcomed the paid distraction
from what felt like another delay to the start of an

actual life, a career, making what I intended to make, but that I was hit by alternating waves of peace and resentment. I told her that I had found myself in a constant temporary state, such that the word *temporary* had lost its soothing, self-professing quality. She said that was too bad. She said that most lives are lived on one long service road running parallel to the one they should be on. People get off their highways to get gas and they end up on a side road or just staying and working at the gas station. She said that she preferred films without any score, that sound can kill an image. It was getting dark. Before she left, she said to never contact her directly. She had excised everything extraneous from her life, she said. Including unnecessary interactions.

In the first weeks of hearing loss, I began to think about the idea of luck—the cheapness and the vastness of the word, its relation to fear. I wrote down a sentence from a summary of *The Histories* (second century B.C.E.), which the Greek chronicler Polybius began writing while being held hostage in a cell in Rome: "When no cause can be discovered for events such as floods, drouts, frosts or even in politics, then the cause of these events may be fairly attributed to luck." I wondered about this adverb, *fairly*.

I began talking to myself out loud to make sure

I had retained the hearing I had left. This was a useless exercise, but I carried on with it anyway. I would say things like *Hello?* at random intervals as though someone had knocked at the door. My voice would always be the one thing I could hear, even if everything else had been shut out. But I could hear my voice more clearly now, and even when I wasn't speaking my thoughts felt somehow louder. I had become nearer to myself.

The phenomenologist Husserl proposes that even in the instant when we speak to ourselves silently, there must be something like a tiny rip that divides us into the speaker and the hearer. This rip somehow separates you from yourself in the moment of hearing yourself speak. *Moment* or *instant* translates in German to *Augenblick*—"blink of the eye." I found that this tiny rip had become, to me, imperceivable.

It was as though the sound I *was* hearing was not the sound itself but rather its ghost. And like a good ghost, the sound made itself known only when it wanted to, flimsily, moving through the room in vacant form before fading or disappearing altogether. While sitting at the dining table, I noticed the street outside was no longer where it had always been, just through the living room window. I found instead that the street was in my kitchen—the hum of passing cars was now coming from somewhere near my stove and sounded like bees.

I met a friend at a small Spanish restaurant around the corner, one that we used to frequent as a group before everyone's hours seemed to be accounted for, the type of place that still uses white tablecloths and stands their napkins up in small pyramids. The waiter stood in front of me reading specials and yet he spoke from behind me. The friend was in a bad mood, and she complained about an issue with her mother, a narcissist whose narcissism had been inflamed by divorce and minor cancer. I can't understand, I said. You don't have to understand everything, she said. Sometimes people just need someone to listen. No, I mean I can't hear you, I said. She laughed through her embarrassment. And sent her paella back—it was *too* fishy.

While doing dishes, I could hear my upstairs neighbor jumping rope. This neighbor always walked a line of disrespect. At 10:00 p.m. on a Sunday? I thought. But when I shut off the water, I found it was the sound of my own heartbeat.

When I blinked, I could hear my eyelids meeting—dull and dense like a head hitting a pillow. The blink and the heartbeat moved in contrapuntal motion. It was like an argument over how time should be divided. Punctuated. Wounded. Like *this*. No, like *that*. While the heart is fairly reliable, the blink is indeterminate—once I paid attention to the blinking, almost every blink surprised me. I could never find a pattern. I thought, in the end, which would have the last word? The blink or the beat?

Overnight, the word *temporary* underwent Easter and resurrected. In September and October, my primary commitment was the movement of a car from one side of the street to the other. Tuesdays and Fridays. The car had been left to me by a friend who had moved to Thessaloniki after suddenly falling in love with a much older woman who worked for the Greek Ministry of Culture. Her father still paid the insurance on the vehicle, a white Saab from the nineties that could be started with a Phillips-head screwdriver. I felt a certain devotion to this car as it was the only thing, other than the little black dog, that depended on me for anything during this period, and I took pleasure and comfort in the simple action—the performance. When the street sweeper passed, I felt as though I had orchestrated its passing.

On the second Tuesday of October, I sat in the car waiting for my cue and remembered shifting gears for my mother when I was around ten as she drove on empty roads outside of the city. A lesson in listening not driving, she said. In this instance, she said my hearing could not be selective. And I remembered feeling that my life and her life depended on my ability to translate the sound into action. I was at the age when you realize that everything can be deadly.

On the third Tuesday of October, the car would not move. Finally a mechanic arrived, a man with the largest hands I've seen to this day, and said not to trust anything that comes back to life. Rid yourself of everything unreliable, he said.

I became close to the word *permanent*. Each day felt more permanent than the previous one. Whatever had fixed itself upon the day before was forged deeper into the following—every shred of life its own nail, and God a translucent hammer . . .

That same month, I had noticed that there was a couple who lived in an apartment across the courtyard—they would lie naked, one on top of the other, each night, unmoving for thirty minutes at a time or longer, overhead light on, the bed perfectly level with the window. It appeared almost like an interrogation room in its fluorescence, but the couple's daily action resisted interpretation.

On Halloween, my ex, a wishful filmmaker who was moving to Los Angeles, came to say hello and goodbye to our once-shared little black dog, and to drop off a small light fixture, not remarkable enough to bring across the country. I had not seen him since we had decided not to speak to each other. He had not yet seen the apartment. He said that the texture of the walls reminded him of Italy. Like stucco. He said that it was perfect for one person. He said that my hair had gotten so long.

Through the window, he witnessed the routine. They are soaking, he said matter-of-factly. He said that it was a loophole around God. That Mormons, before marriage, can be inside each other only as long as they are perfectly still. Then God will have no idea. I had to ask the filmmaker to enunciate. That night, I was losing some words. He sat in the white chair with his black shoes on, breathing.

The filmmaker said that he had, as a teenager, for one summer, dated the daughter of the second wife of Marcel Marceau. I knew this already, of course. At the time, the girl had just ended a relationship with a Mormon. In the late 1980s, the girl's mother, a mime in her own right, had provided bodily preparation for Roman Polanski for his role as Gregor Samsa in *The Metamorphosis* of Kafka at Théâtre du Gymnase. The same year, she appeared in *Frantic* directed by Polanski as "the attendant in the toilets"—she had even helped develop the concept of Bip the Clown, he said as he left, and I thanked him for the lamp. Feel better, he said.

Eventually, The Soakers left and were replaced by a cat and a woman, my age, who had a fanatical tick. She ran one hand through her hair, lifted it straight up to the sky, and offered a quick twirl at the end of each lift. I always thought that she was exercising a very specific muscle by performing this gesture for most of the day. And I felt nostalgia for those months with The Soakers, for no other reason than that they had passed and I had found myself performing this same violent action with my hair.

In the mornings, I had a new routine. Over decaffeinated coffee, I thought about my profession. I was incapable of specificity. I would think in big sweeping thoughts. I thought about what I would still like to profess. I thought about what was foreclosed and what wasn't. I thought about the slow drain of my bank account like a leak that was unaccounted for— the caulking! I thought about making something of nothing. I thought about making nothing of nothing. And finally, nothing of something. Each presented its own challenge. I used to love challenge, I thought. I thought variations of these thoughts while removing the stray hairs from the edge of the sink or applying lotion or emptying out things from the fridge that had gone bad or checking to see if I had received a text message or wondering what I should be doing or *would* be doing in that very moment. For a period I expected to open my email to a congratulatory notice or an invitation or an acceptance letter (though I'd applied to nothing). Everything represented something else.

It was required that my hearing be monitored closely. My treatment was a work of improvisation.

Like jazz, or the preparation of a meal using ingredients already in the fridge. When I asked the doctor about possible outcomes, he said my expectations for treatment should be like those of a person engaged in an extramarital affair. Nonexistent. This way, he explained, any successes could be celebrated as unexpected wins.

In November, I began to go for weekly hearing tests. I received compensation for my participation, a relief from the steady leak—which would have been a point of concern had I been capable at that time of entertaining any additional concerns. Just outside of the station by the off-site hospital facility was an industrial building that occupied the whole block. On top of the building sat a large sign that read JOHN'S CAGES in a bold yellow serif and then in fine text: *Under the directorship of former Major Leaguer and World Series Champion John Rodriguez, indoor baseball facility offering batting cage rentals and private hitting, pitching, and fielding instruction.* An adjacent sign displayed nothing but a fat yellow arrow pointing downward. Only the arrow was visible from the waiting room window. Above the arrow were nothing but brilliant clouds—as though the sky were downloading to Earth. Next to this window, inside the waiting room, was a chart of the sign language alphabet that doubled as an advertisement for the Gotham Sign School: 212-570-0075.

Around this time, the people who called or wrote to me regularly—the general circle of friends who had drifted close and far, collected over twenty-seven years—seemed to volatilize. When something becomes constant it stops being urgent. Only my mother and the friend in Thessaloniki continued reaching out, and I wondered what sort of suffering had led this friend to feel pain on my behalf. On the phone, voices were narrower, as if funneled through a tin can.

One night, when I returned my concerned mother's phone call, she spoke about a dying friend, a woman who had come over for dinner often when I was very young. My mother insisted that I call her before she died. Call for me, she said, do it for me, she said like a mother, before saying good night. When I called the dying friend the next day, she answered, but she told me she could not talk for long because she had the runs from her chemo. She said it was terrible that I would go deaf at my age, and I said it was terrible she would die at hers. She laughed and said she would rather die than go deaf.

I told her it had all started at the very end of August, the 29th, and she said that was funny, it was the day John Cage first turned his piece *4′33″* over to the public at The Maverick, the little outdoor concert hall right up her road in Woodstock. She said that coincidence was a religion and that she was agnostic.

She had volunteered at The Maverick several summers in a row, in the eighties. The manager was arrogant, she said, and she still avoided him like the plague at the health food store. The date, August 29, had been drilled into her head for the short informational monologue she gave to visitors who were often failed artists.

She excused herself and returned to the phone many minutes later. She said that she had gone to a conservative all-girls preparatory high school in Virginia and that Merce Cunningham had grown up with her headmaster in Centralia. He came to the school to perform for the girls. Cage joined; they weren't ever apart. She said that Merce choreographed a piece for them and that John made a score using pieces of plywood he had found in the back of their auditorium, that he drew the musical staff across the planks and where the knots and lines hit the staff would determine the notes in the piece.

The dying friend alternated between calling him Cage and John. She said that Cage thought of silence only as a state of mind—a question of intention and non-intention. They were just a bunch of half-baked Southern schoolgirls but they could understand him, she said, somehow everything he and Merce said and did made sense and it was then that she decided she wanted to be a dancer, to move to New York, et cetera, et cetera, et cetera. She said that John said silence is nothing but the things we choose to ignore and exclude, and that he left empty space in the music so he could show the listener that it was not actually empty, just subject to the whims of chance.

She had moved to New York to join Cunningham's company as an understudy but nothing ever came of her dance career. She said it was odd that she ended up in Woodstock all those years later. She said that day when John spoke to them he told them about the performance at The Maverick.

She said the player had placed the sheet music on the piano and pulled a small clock out from his pocket. He lifted the cover over the piano keys and looked down at his clock. He began a dance with his eyes, glancing from clock to sheet music, tracing the time. After thirty-three seconds had passed, he opened the piano cover, which marked the conclusion of the first movement. He then closed the cover and again resumed the back-and-forth glances between sheet and clock. This time for two minutes and forty seconds. For the final movement, which lasted one minute and twenty seconds, she said that he repeated the action and then opened the piano, picked up his stopwatch and sheet music, rose to his feet, and exited the stage.

She said that he had placed a time frame around a series of consecutive moments, forcing the listener to hear whatever was happening around them within that frame of time. She said that it is when we shift our attention to the frame that we are reminded of the frame's purpose—to exclude, to make an inside and outside. At the same time, he was running away from the preexisting frame, she said. The attempt to escape the frame only leads to the expansion of the frame. We end up drudging more of life back into the frame of art.

It's not unlike Duchamp's ready-mades, she said. You get it, she said. John never actually talked about ready-mades but he did talk about Duchamp's paintings on glass. You can see through the work to what's not in the work, through to what lies outside, where there is no such thing as empty space or empty time . . . She stopped abruptly, she had to go. She really had to go but hoped for a miracle, for one or both of us.

It was not too late after we got off, 10:00 p.m., and so I did the dishes. I had developed the habit of making tea and not drinking it. Small swamp waters multiplied on every hard surface of the apartment. I collected them when I ran out of mugs and let the cycle begin again. I walked the dog around the block three times. She often failed to perform her duties, distracted by the rats. She was often constipated. This was a surprise to me, given the unchanging nature of her diet and routine. Our lives felt more similar now. A dog's life. She seemed to be growing less interested in me.

When I called my mother back to let her know that I had fulfilled her wish, she thanked me. I asked if she had been to The Maverick—she had lived in Woodstock working as an equine vet for farms across Ulster County in the 1980s. She said that she had been to The Maverick, once by accident when she had been summoned in the middle of the night to perform an emergency house call at a horse farm owned by a notorious, high-ranking member of the mob. A horse was under distress, experiencing severe colic.

She had visited the farm two times before to perform routine visits. They owned nine Clydesdales and one black Arabian. But since she had last visited, the mobster whom she had dealt with directly had appeared on the cover of the *New York Post* and his twin sons had taken charge of the farm. I thought of Laocoön and his twin sons. She said that there were always people working on the telephone poles at the end of the road, and she had always assumed they were members or affiliates of the Federal Bureau of Investigation.

When she arrived that night at 3:00 a.m., she was greeted first by two guards in suits with small handguns who said, Good evening, miss, in their southwest-Brooklyn accents. She was then received

by the sons with their chenille sweatsuits and luxuri-
ant black eyebrows. They walked her around a stone
building with flashlights to the paddock where the
black Arabian was lying on its side. He's not going
to die, is he? one asked. She told them that in these
cases the intestines can become twisted and it's then
that the body shuts down. The only way to avoid this
was to walk the horse and not let him stop moving
for several hours. They agreed that they couldn't afford to have this horse die on their watch and offered
her a generous hourly fee to stay through the morning to see the horse live. She felt she had no choice
but to agree. My mother is a beautiful woman with
flat-black hair, small, strong, and thin—like a black
Arabian but opposite.

She said she stayed up all night walking this
mobster's horse through the field in figure eights.
Trailing fifty feet behind her was one of the men
with guns, who said nothing all night. When they
got near the far end of the paddock, she thought
she heard whistling that sounded almost like wind,
but the night was still. She noticed a cluster of light
between the trees. This paddock went deep over a
little ridge to the far edge of the property. As she approached the light, she realized what she had heard
were many flutes playing at once and, eventually,
she saw an audience sitting on wooden benches facing a stage beneath an open-faced wooden structure

with a Dutch roof. On the stage were more than twenty players, and hanging across a rafter was a banner that said ANNUAL 24-HOUR PANNALAL GHOSH – BANSURI MARATHON. She walked the horse in circles and listened until the sun came up and the man with the gun stayed fifty feet behind her leaning on a tree. She said the horse had survived and that driving home the next morning she realized that it was The Maverick that bordered the mobster's farm.

She asked what I had made myself for dinner (a white fish) and thanked me again for calling the dying friend. She will die very soon, she said like a prophet. She used to give you baths when you were young, she said, and hung up. By this time, no voice was familiar, but I could distinguish them by the rhythm of a sentence. Her statements had sounded like questions.

I began to feel that sensation one has on trains or in cars, the specific feeling of standing still while moving. I began to keep track of every little thing, as if it were something to solve, in a small black notebook. I wrote down a list of what I had eaten that day (frozen blueberries, baby spinach, rice noodles, bread) and the number of phone calls I'd made (two), what I had worn, the pills I had taken.

I received an email asking if I was available for work—a score for a film about the disappearance of a young woman studying abroad in Hokkaido, mainly chimes, wind instruments, bells—no, not at this time, I'm afraid I am too busy, I said. I went to the hardware store to purchase the ear coverings used around power tools—to control the quiet. I had received my first check in the mail for my participation in the trial. I stopped buying anything other than groceries and toiletries. I bought one nice pair of black Japanese wool pants, used, in October. And a five-pack of new plain black cotton underwear. Occasionally, I bought a movie ticket. I kept score in the little black book . . .

As I was stepping into the shower, the friend in Thessaloniki called. I was already naked. For her, it was very early in the morning and for me very late at night. She asked how I was. She only ever called while in transit, so there were always so many sounds in the background and wind, which is always so violent over the phone.

I told her I believed that the distinct unhappiness I was feeling was payback for a childhood that had been distinctly happy. I told her I often thought about whether I would prefer a happy childhood or a happy adulthood—if that option had been extended to me like a choice of meal on an airplane. The answer seemed obvious, but then I thought about it and it was no longer clear what I would choose. She said she had to go, that she had just seen a dog get hit by a blue car.

In the following weeks, apathy became a kind of tranquility. A holiday from impulse. The barrenness of my daily landscape made distant things feel recent. A vacation in Central America, a master's degree, work, love I'd felt, incidents, accidents, the nothings that comprise a life. Now I was making a score by keeping score. Sometimes I forgot I was sick because the sickness was so clean. So odorless. Efficient. Quiet. No more alcohol, caffeine, chocolate, mushrooms, salt, meat, dairy. Doctor's orders.

Walking back to the train after the next hearing test, I found that John's Cages occupied the entire ground-floor space of the building with the advertisement and the yellow downward arrow. I pictured a series of soundless chambers inside—like the prayer rooms found in airports. As I walked back to the train, through the glass bricks, I could make out small bodies tossing and catching the balls—like little silences, white dots of nothing shifting in air. It was clear to me then that what I feared was losing the variations of silence. It became clearer to me that the fear was the frame of my body. It became clearer still that the fear was not being able to see, so to speak, through the glass.

I received a text message from the friend in Thessaloniki saying that the dog had died in the accident. She said that she always seemed to witness accidents. That she was a regular bystander. How would you define an accident? I asked her. Hours later, she wrote back saying that she would define an accident as a patient thing . . . an addendum to air, like a gas that hangs and binds with a feeling and then transforms into a bag of invisible bricks. How the bricks fall, and how we interpret their falling, that is the luck . . . I responded that in my happy childhood there had been interludes of unhappiness related inextricably to "the falling of bricks." Childhood is an abject state common to everyone, she replied.

It was almost December and I had started to find that the word *silence* ran to me out of pages and spoken sentences. It wanted my attention—a desperate sort of flirtation. I began to note simple and unremarkable patterns around the word, such as that *seeing, staring, hanging,* or *watching* are often coupled with silence. That the adverb *completely* often precedes *silent*. That the verb *fall* often precedes *silent*. That the architecture of silence is the gaze. That silence is without transition. That silence is dressed as an injury.

I sat in the eight-by-ten-foot living room at the end of each day, when the blood always rushed inward, leaving the walls pale like one of the Hammershøi paintings of his apartment at Strandgade 30, which always seemed to ask: How could a room alone hold the fear of being *overlooked by God in this enormous household*? I took more prednisone.

The filmmaker wrote to recommend a movie—it was showing in midtown for one night only, part of a series. I was not so accustomed to doing things alone—the movies, the dinners in restaurants, the shopping. I started just staying home, which made it tolerable, the being alone, and sometimes allowed me to forget about it altogether. The movie was about a father, a widower, who is losing his daughter to marriage. Men talk over sake at different watering holes about losing things and war. The film is Japanese and had originally been renamed for its American release after a type of mackerel, a tasteless fish, served in autumn. There is no reference to mackerel or eating a fish in the film, but the movie itself was meant to convey the quiet flavor of the fish.

In the film were many shots that were like still lifes, cutaways to objects. Often the shots came in threes and were accompanied by music. It was a

Tuesday, the first very cold day of the season. There was an empty threat of snow. I took the subway home from the theater. In my car, a woman had a rip right down the back of her stockings that revealed a slice of her bare leg—a small silence had broken her outfit. She held the metal pole with one hand and a red patent bag with the other and with sleepy eyes stared out of the train window. Many people stared at the rip, some out of pity, some pleasure, others both. And there I saw it, silence vulnerable to more than just sound.

Later, at home, under the covers, window rattling, I decided that silence is having too much time on your hands—now that I had absolutely nothing to do other than live. Silence is when someone says, Actually don't come, and you tell them you're already here, waiting downstairs.

Each day was an exercise in disbelief and I would wake up and wish to be renovated. What went on in the night? I was always disappointed that no progress had been made. Whenever it rained, I remembered the sound of rain hitting the air conditioner.

In the mornings I often thought about my mother saying to me once that the self-proclaimed busiest women she knew did not have jobs. That simple tasks like replacing light bulbs, making phone calls, filling out forms, and scheduling dental appointments—tasks that the working woman is forced to fit into stolen minutes—become very dire for the nonworking woman. I thought, Now *I* am a busy woman.

On my way to the next hearing test, I held the door for the woman who lived below me. She had a face and hair that changed often—her eye color seemed to be the only constant. Her lipstick defied the barrier of her lips as if to say, no these are where the lips go—a land survey for the face. The jump roper had told me that this woman had been a dancer at Bada Bing!, the fictional strip club in Lodi, New Jersey, from *The Sopranos*. She was moving boxes to the street one by one when she said she had a proposal for me. She followed me back onto the sidewalk. She said that she was in the process of freeing herself. That as a result she wanted me to have her storage unit for a fair fee. In the building, there were only studio apartments and a few one-bedrooms, all of which lacked closets.

She said her storage unit was just a mausoleum for her two Italian greyhounds—S and M—who had died within days of each other. What remained? Their toys, clothing, and other items used in relation to them, like retractable gates—she never had children because she had hated her mother. When the dogs had played, she said, they would chase each other in circles and often become one beautiful silver sphere that looked like it was floating. Like the event horizon of a black hole. Occasionally they were very violent with each other. Like any siblings. We've all almost killed someone, she said. That's a fact about being alive. I thought then of the woman whose dog was killed in the courtyard in *Rear Window* and who shouts out into the night, "Did you kill him because he liked you?" I thought of the limp dog being raised up in the wicker basket.

I told her I was an only child. She said there is never only one of anything. That I was just the thing to survive the passage from nonphysical to physical. That I was part of a continuum of children that were versions of myself created by my parents. She told me that she had, along with another tenant on the second floor, suspected that I was a well-known actress. That he had told her that he knew me from somewhere, that he had seen me in things. That I was being modest. That this was just a pied-à-terre and that was why she never saw me around. That I kept to myself for privacy. A low profile. She said that I looked to her like a young Jacqueline Onassis with a smaller forehead and more life in the lips, and like her brother's wife's sister who worked in precious metals prior to suffering an aneurysm. When I told her I was not an actress, she did not believe me.

She said that she was herself an actress, too, but that she had retired to be a better mother to the dogs. She loved to act but did not like taking direction from men. She had realized that at the end of the day, life was made for pleasure and most people chose to deny themselves this because they didn't know that they were free. Her cousins in Greece took out loans to go on vacation, she said. They were people who understood life's value. Even poor people had island homes in Greece. Their economy was the way it was because Greeks chose pleasure. She clarified that she was more Dionysian and less Apollonian. That she was Greek by marriage but actually Sicilian by way of New Jersey. She told me she was in training to become a life coach.

She asked me not to tell anyone about the offer of the storage unit, that the woman above her had asked many times for the unit but that I seemed like someone who would give it back if she changed her mind whereas the other woman did not. She said with horror that she suspected this woman worked in marketing. She said that she gravitated toward people who had a hard time maintaining close relationships. She said she would like to keep a key as well as the fifteen dollars per month up front for the entire year. That she was trustworthy. That if she ever had to hide, that was where she would hide. That it was impossible to find anyone down there. That one must always both seek out and collect hiding places. You never know when you will have to hide, she said. I was late.

In the waiting room, my name was called out and

I followed the audiologist down the white hall. He stopped before a black door covered in notes and drawings by children and a plaque that read ROBERT WALTHER, PHD – AUDIOLOGY. Days before, in bed, I had been reading a book titled *A Little Ramble* written by a group of visual artists in response to the work of Robert Walser, a writer whom artists always embarrassingly seem to think belongs to them like a secret. In the collection are excerpts from conversations between Walser and Carl Seelig, a friend who often visited him in the asylum where he spent his last decades. They went on long walks together through the Appenzell.

In one entry, he recalls walking with Walser through Gossau, where they witnessed a procession of altar boys across the field in red coats "radiant as geraniums." From Gossau, the pair travels to Oberbüren and, at last, they arrive at a forked wooded path where Walser insists upon turning left—"the right path often leads to the wrong things, and the wrong path to the right things." They arrive at a small house, where they find these words painted on the front door:

> Good luck or bad
> Take them in stride
> Both shall pass
> As will you

I sat on a small wooden stool. As he secured head-phones over my ears as well as magnets on the bones behind my ears, I asked Robert Walther if he had ever heard of Robert Walser. I have not, he said, and shut the door.

You will hear a man's voice and he will tell you what to say, said Robert Walther on the other side of the glass.

Say the word *love*.

Love.

Say the word *hash*.

Hash.

Say the word *sunset*.

Sunset.

Say the word *dust*.

Dust.

Say the word *chalk*.

Chalk.

Say the word *sweat*.

Sweat.

Say the word *lot*.

Lot.

Then another man entered the booth and now he too watched me through the glass.

Say the word *jail*.

Jail.

Say the word *joy*.

Joy.

Say the word *wince*.
Wince.
Say the word *want*.
Want.
Say the word *war*.
War.
Say the word *cake*.
Cake.
Say the word *lawyer*.
Lawyer.
Say the word *drone*.
Drone.
Say the word *tear*.
Tear.
You've got a great imagination, said the other man in the booth.
Thank you, I said.
Then both men left the booth.
Hello? I said.
I wanted to tell Robert Walther and his colleague to leave words out of this. This was about sound, not words. I would always have words . . .

In the mornings, after the decaffeinated coffee, after walking the little black dog, I would choose one song to play on a loop throughout the day. I would play the song so quietly that it was almost inaudible and the song would be suspended in the air like a circling fly—a low humming. Eventually, I began to think of songs as flies—the living anagram of files . . .

The daily listening exercise served a dual purpose. Since each day was a rehearsal for the next, I was preparing for everything to be the quietest version of itself before disappearing altogether, in a cloak of itself.

I began to acquaint myself with mishearing. In primary school, I had a French teacher who taught using photographs that only she herself had taken—*Nothing from the books!* She would narrate in both French and English. When we studied the architecture of Paris, she projected photographs she had taken in the early eighties of a boat tour down the Seine with her partner, Vivienne. In one image, a guide pointed up toward the roof of Notre Dame. She told us that if you *squeeeent*, really *squeeeent*, you can see the famous Apple Sauce. It was fifteen years later when the cathedral went up in flames that I understood and experienced the delayed pleasure in my mishearing. A news headline read: "The Apostles LIVE—removed from the roof only days before the fire."

I kept score. Now I ate all of my meals standing up. Now I took my showers hot. Now I only wore my hair back in a loose attempt at a braid. Now I took a long time to respond to things if at all. Now I moisturized my face with a thick beeswax cream that made it look like a polished shoe. Now I looked younger—my cheeks were round and bright from the steroids. I had transient tremors. Little earthquakes of the body. Now I was a mint-tea person. Someone I barely knew, a dramaturge, wrote to ask—*How is the trial going?* She had heard from the mutual friend in Thessaloniki about my situation. Both her parents were born deaf. Did I want their email addresses?

The trial—I thought of silences in court. I thought of pleading the fifth. Especially in the mornings, I thought, I am a criminal. I thought, this is grand larceny. What is more valuable than time? I was being held at my own border.

I thought, This is an affair. Once you cheat, you cheat again. And now this was business as usual. This was how it would be until it wasn't. I switched to cod, which cost less than sole. I switched to drugstore shampoo and conditioner. I stopped treating myself to occasional flowers from the bodega. I started drinking Nescafé (decaf).

On the last day of November, a full-body interior inspection was ordered—a search for indicators and signs of inflammation elsewhere. When I arrived for the procedure, the nurse came in and told me I had to lock up my phone and rings and necklace and asked if I was having anesthesia. It was a question I did not have the answer to. There was an older man, a tuba player with an esophagus in need of repair, being prepared for his operation next to me. He was very talkative and then he was quiet like a small child in the back seat of a car suddenly overcome by sleep. He was taken away and replaced with a blond woman who was very pregnant. She looked my age and like a bird. She complimented each nurse's appearance one by one: nails, watches, footwear. You get better care this way, she said. She was having twins.

She told me that her grandfather had worked for the state department in the 1950s and that her grandmother had given birth to her mother in a rural Italian hospital. In the hospital, her grandmother had shared a room with Ingrid Bergman. It was a baby Isabella Rossellini and her twin that came out of Bergman. The grandmother and Bergman became close in those hours they spent next to each other in the hospital but never saw each other again. Ten years ago, she said, her mother was at a farm stand on Long Island, buying ears of corn, when she saw Isabella Rossellini there, also buying corn, sunflowers, blackberries, with wet hair and a yellow dog. She went over to her and identified herself—she said they were born in the same room on the same day and Rossellini said she'd heard about her mother, Mary, from her mother, Ingrid. Rossellini apparently hugged her and said, If only we also had traded our lives . . .

In the procedure room was a sign that read, YOU ARE AMAZING. The doctor told me to lie on my side. He told me to take a deep breath in and to hold the air until he told me to release it. They opened the gown from behind and, as the camera entered me, the doctor called me *a professional*.

That night, at home, I read about Bergman and I learned that she was born and died on the same day: August 29. This date seemed to follow me, and to precede me. It was that same day, thirty-six years later, that I woke up to leave for the wedding in Venice, the same day that *4′33″* premiered at The Maverick. On that day in 1982 at midnight, Bergman's sixty-seventh birthday, she died in London. I read that her ex-husband and three other people were there when she died, that they had drunk their last toast to her hours earlier. That there was a copy of *The Little Prince* on her bedside table, opened to a page near the end—the page where one of those deadly yellow snakes is waiting at the foot of the wall on which the little prince sits when the narrator shoots him with a revolver: "The snake let himself flow easily across the sand like the dying spray of a fountain, and, in no apparent hurry, disappeared, with a light metallic sound, among the stones."

Bergman's memorial service was held in October with twelve hundred mourners in attendance. I thought of a scene from *Journey to Italy*—her screen husband helps her get her coat on and she says, "I don't think you're happy when we're alone." And he replies, "Are you sure you know when I'm happy?" "Ever since we left for this trip I'm not so sure . . ." she says.

I wrote to the filmmaker to tell him about the co-occurrences but he ignored what I had said and instead asked if I was feeling up to seeing a show of paintings by a childhood friend of his the following day. He said that his things had been shipped, keys returned to the landlord, and he would be staying on a series of couches for the coming weeks until his departure. I was not sure whether this was a couched request for my couch to be included in the series. I did not offer it, but I agreed to see the show.

The next morning, I was thirty minutes late to the gallery and he'd already walked through the show and said he had to leave shortly for a reason he didn't offer. I had always considered myself to be a respectful person but the filmmaker had historically made me feel like a disrespectful person. I told him this once and he replied that my feelings were my own. That he couldn't *make me* feel anything. I did not apologize for my lateness.

The filmmaker's childhood friend was known for painting his name over and over again onto imposing canvases. By the entrance was the press release

and a printout of a recent interview with the artist. Toward the end of the interview they stopped
talking about the paintings and ceramics and the
interviewer asked the artist if he thought he was im-
proving as a person. The artist responded by saying
he thought he was a much worse person but that also
perhaps he was just a hurt person. The artist said
he thought he had a good heart, that he was a loving person, that he would do anything for anybody
but that he'd been hurt by people. That people had
been cruel to him. (The painter was very successful
at a young age.) He agreed with the interviewer that
forgiving people is something we do for ourselves.
I watched the filmmaker move around the empty
room. He walked over and asked me if I was going
to look at the paintings or just read the interview,
which I could read at home. It was at that moment,
on the other side of the gallery, that a woman began
apologizing profusely and her apologies rang out
throughout the space.

She said that she was so sorry. She said that she
felt horrible. She said that she was so embarrassed.
I was looking right at the filmmaker as the apologies rang out and it was as though she were speaking
for one of us. As though these words hung in the air
waiting to be claimed.

And then another woman's voice joined in and
said not to worry. She said, Please don't worry at all.

She said, Don't worry, it's not your fault. She said, It's not your fault at all. She said that it's not anyone's fault. It went on like that and the filmmaker looked at me and smiled till they fell silent. He said he had to run. He set a hand on my back and then removed it as if he'd touched a hot pan.

The interviewer asked the artist if he thought he'd have kids. He said no. He said you don't get big love in your thirties like you do in your twenties. It's hard to have close friends as an adult, he said. He said that everyone is out of town or recovering from some dramatic thing.

When I went to leave, I found one of the women bent over with a bottle of bleach spraying a trail of it onto the concrete floor, from the door to a bench, where the other woman sat removing dog shit from a space in her shoe that divided the big toe from the rest like the hoof of a pitch-black goat.

On the first day of December, I was given a higher dose of prednisone. Small, white, dissolvable circular attempts at keeping the inflammation at bay. Time was marked by doses not days. Measured in weight—the common milligram. I quickly learned that sick-time is to be acutely outside of time but acutely aware of its passage.

Each dose of prednisone got a room of its own on

the page in the little black notebook where I had previously noted things I was meant to do—the hours I was meant to arrive certain places. The people I was meant to see. But now, there was nothing I was meant to do other than these numbers. I was arriving at numbers and leaving numbers behind and meeting them again. Forty and 16.5 were two numbers I seemed to meet often.

I fixated on the work of the artist Hanne Darboven, a Hamburger, and heir to the Darboven coffee empire. (For this reason alone, I pictured Darboven counting coffee beans—moving beans from one black bucket into one blue bucket, one bean at a time.) She lived in New York City for two years in the 1960s before returning to Germany, where she stayed until her death in 2009. In New York City, she had undergone friendlessness.

She had studied as a classical pianist before taking up minimalism as though it were a piano. When she got home, she devised her Konstruktionen, a neutral and artificial language made up of only lines and numbers. Her language of numbers allowed her to track time's bend in a specific, orderly way according to her own system. She liked that something unspeakable was universal. She considered herself a writer not an artist. She said it often: I am a writer not an artist. She filled pages and then walls with her systems.

There's one piece from 1981 called *Wende >80< . . .* *Wende* translates to "turning point." For the first time, she took her numbers and turned them into notes. Translating her translations. There are images too. I wondered why in 1981 she turned and what turned her.

Wende.

Wende.

Wende.

I hoped each day for a *wende*. This word to me sounded like its meaning. *Wende*. My tongue became addicted to this word. No, I did not want the English *wend*, I did not want to meander. I did not want to find my way. I did not want to wind. I wanted my way to be found. I wanted the German *wende*.

Tapering by 0.5 milligrams every five stable days. At first, I filled in my future with doses until there were no doses at all. This was what optimism looked like. But my doses without fail stood still or moved me backward, setting me back in time—sometimes I was set back by whole months in just one day. Eventually, I stopped filling in my future with doses because I finally understood that each dose was a revision of the previous dose. Like a day. And you cannot revise a day that has yet to take place.

IN THE TREE right outside my apartment window, a red dog leash appeared, looped and hanging like an empty noose. It circled a small patch of sky. It remained there for the month of December and part of January.

I had a follow-up appointment with the doctor who had commented about the human ability to reach the moon—the one who recommended abstaining from anything that might give way to heightened emotions, from weddings to surprise celebrations, unexpected deaths to orgasms. The thing is . . . he said, and then he didn't finish his sentence.

Never mind, he said. Do you remember? he said. Do you remember a heightened moment before your hearing dropped? He said to keep a log of "moments of elevation." Somehow we arrived at the particular pleasure that comes from finding something you didn't realize had even been lost. Articles of clothing, clarity, house keys. I kept score . . .

I explained that a fear had settled in me—that someday, the words I spoke would somehow be different from the words I was thinking—that I would have nothing but faith to confirm that I was saying what I intended to say.

He asked if I would be interested in entering a hypnotherapy trial—a potential palliative care. The clinical hypnotherapist who was conducting the trial was based in Bolinas and would be interested in practicing the hypnosis via video conference each day for one hour over the course of two weeks. I agreed to a consultation session.

I met the hypnotherapist two days later, in the evening, on the screen. Behind him was a green parrot in a white cage, Frida, a rescue macaw, born, I learned, with no voice box and therefore not suited for the wild. It was for this reason only that he did not feel sorry keeping her in the cage. We began with small talk. I sat in the white chair. He asked if I had heard of the musician Suzanne Ciani. He told me she was his neighbor there in Bolinas. And not just a neighbor in the loose sense. Their properties touched. The referring doctor had told him that I was also a musician . . . Sometimes he could hear her digital arpeggios drifting into his window! But not today . . . not today . . . he said. The wind was blowing north . . .

We reached the subject of my ears. I tried to explain the rolling thunder—It's like God adjusting his piano stool but never getting around to the song. He took sporadic notes. He asked if I believed in God. No, I told him. He said he practiced the Ericksonian method—a method that uses indirect suggestion, metaphor, storytelling.

He had what I assumed were many degrees hanging on his wall behind him, next to the parrot and the cage. But through the screen, the frames on the wall appeared empty, suspended only by Northern Californian sunlight. He had a sheerness about him. Very pale blue eyes and thin white hair. As the session went on the light began to erase him too. Our session was broken up by a poor connection and so I never felt I entered any state other than the one I was already in.

Alone in the room again, I remembered reading that a horse and a fish, or a horse and a man, or even two men compared to each other, do not have the same capacity to be affected. That they are not affected by the same things, or not affected by the same things in the same way. And I thought this about my days, that previously one day had been a horse and the next day had been a fish and each day itself had had a changed capacity to be affected, always in relation to other days. Now all of my days just felt like fish.

I had begun to understand my own life by misinterpreting things I was reading and experiencing with only half of my attention. I found clarity in misinterpretation. And I thought that our misinterpretations are perhaps the most individual and specific things we have.

The following day, we met again—this time thirty minutes later. The sun had already begun to set and the hypnotherapist was just a solid dark mass. Could I see him, or was he sitting dangerously close to his own shadow? I can't seem to get out of it! he said. He added that he didn't usually hold sessions at this time of day and that perhaps he should invest in a window treatment or tack up one of his wife's many sarongs. I told him that I could only see his silhouette but that it was fine by me. He apologized profusely for the poor connection and now *this*. I told him I was used to poor connections.

He said it was funny that I mentioned poor connections. He listened to The Buzzer sometimes for hours a day. I told him I did not know what he was referring to.

He leaned in to the screen. He said it was a radio station no one claims to run. The Petersburg Popper. The Soviet Sonata. The Commie Contata. MDZhB. It had broadcast a low shortwave frequency from somewhere north of Moscow since at least 1982.

He said that if you tune your radio to 4625 kHz from anywhere on Earth, you can pick up the transmissions. Most of the time, all you can hear is a low, long, buzzing drone, but what you listen for is the occasional anomaly—faint words, names, numbers, and, rarely, one side of a conversation—picked up in the background, cutting in and out.

He said that these occurrences suggest that the buzzing tones are not internally generated but rather transmitted from a device placed behind a perpetually live and open microphone. He said that the buzzing tones are believed to be generated by the tone wheel of a 1970s Hammond organ due to their irregular pitch.

He said that last month several unusual broadcasts were observed; these included portions of the buzzer being replaced with extracts from Tchaikovsky's *Swan Lake* and, in one instance, the sound of a woman screaming. He explained that he and his wife, a painter, would tune in while playing mah-jongg in the evenings and sometimes while doing the crossword. It had become a daily ritual. An addiction even! Their

long games were soundtracked by the low drone—
like the drone of a foghorn calling a faraway ship. He
asked if I had seen the film *July Rain*. He said that the
score was made up of constantly flipping radio sta-
tions. I told him I had seen the first fifteen minutes.
I told him that for a week now I had felt like I was
just outside of a station's range. The signal had been
cutting in and out, so to speak, and a perpetual static
had arrived and stayed with me—like a radio station
no one claims to run.

Finally, he asked me to close my eyes. For several moments he said nothing, then, That's right, he
said, as if responding to something I'd said though
I had said nothing . . . And fortunately, he said . . . I
have had some experience with signals . . . with
letting the outside world drift . . . He said, Let the
outside world drift from your awareness . . . as you
grow more comfortable . . . with each breath you
exhale . . . you can remember to forget . . . that the
world outside . . . is outside . . . and then the world
inside . . . is so much more important . . . it really . . .
doesn't matter . . . that today . . . is a new day . . .
a day you've never experienced before . . . you can
rediscover . . . and enjoy the newness . . . as you experience yourself . . . differently . . . because you are
different . . . you know more now . . . and all that you
have learned . . . has taught you . . . how to learn . . .
how to control the dial . . . how to learn . . . a simple

idea . . . that was so easy . . . to forget . . . until now . . . when you discover . . . what can serve you now . . . in the way that you would like . . . It went on like that. And I fell asleep. And neither of us noticed until he stopped talking and the absence of his voice woke me up. Like when someone comes and turns off a light when you're already sleeping and the darkness wakes you. The hypnotherapist said that next time, in order to benefit from the session, I needed to stay awake. I decided to go on and let this man take time from my days—my time was there for the taking.

After the session, I visited the open-source website dedicated to The Buzzer. I found the table where listeners added to a log of overheard words and other notable deviations from the usual drone. On that day, one listener had logged that the station was interrupted by a third-party transmission, likely sent by French fishermen.

Words on the log included:

ГЕЛЬ – gel

ТИМЕЙКА – a word with no real meaning

ДИНГИ – dinghy

БАПТИСТСКИЙ – Baptist

КУХОННЫЙ – a word associated with
   kitchen furniture

БЕЗДОЖДЬ – rainlessness

ГРУЗИНСКИЙ – Georgian

АЙОВА – Iowa

ИЗНОС – exhaustion

ЗАБОРЧИК – diminutive of fence

ЕРЕСЬ – heresy

ЗЕМЛЕВЕД – farming specialist

БАЛКОННЫЙ – belonging to a balcony

АТОМОВКУС – atomic taste

КЕПЛЕР – Johannes Kepler, famous astronomer

ДАЛЬНОСТЬ – distance

КАЗАЧОК – a Cossack folk dance

Who was listening? I pictured versions of myself, alone, in different bodies and foreign rooms at tables leaning over small radios. The sun, setting or rising. I pictured myself extending the antennae as close to the sky as possible, moving nearer to windows, propping them open with miscellaneous objects on hand. I saw it then, listening as sport—like fishing, or masturbation, it takes a certain type of attention. There is that compulsive element too, tied up with fear. Fear of missing a word or a string of them. Are listeners the people who live lives waiting for clues? I thought of a very short essay by Georges Perec about a recurring dream in which he discovers a room in his tiny apartment that he somehow hadn't known existed.

I sat in the sun with my little black dog, who had

developed an acute licking habit. I let her lick me until it was unbearable.

In the next session, I asked the hypnotherapist how it was possible that I could be experiencing such extreme degrees of fear and boredom at once. Forms of fear I had experienced before were engaging. I told him this was a disengaging strain of fear. He asked me if I felt I was waiting for something. I said yes, it felt like I was waiting for a scene in a film I had seen many times. Yes, it was exhausting to live with this level of anticipation. And what I was anticipating was nothingness. This made it all the more exhausting. I told him then that my days felt like exercises.

I had, during this period, taken to grocery shopping at the earliest possible hour—before the music was turned on, before the rush of commuters and caregivers and full-time mothers with small children. One morning, after being told to eat more white fish, due to a vitamin D deficiency from the diuretic, I arrived at 7:00 a.m. to purchase my dinner. There was only one other shopper. As I looked down at all of the fish on ice, I tried to remember the last time I had swum in the sea. When the stranger next to me sneezed, I suddenly remembered—it had been at the Rockaways—and said *love you* instead of *bless you* like the words had just been there waiting to come out. The stranger looked up, nodded, and pointed at the fish I had planned to take through the glass. I watched it disappear as it was wrapped in white paper.

In the following session, I asked the hypnotherapist if he had ever contributed to the log.

He said that he'd had beginner's luck—his first and only log dated back to Christmas Eve, 1997—at that point, he had been a listener for two months.

The Buzzer had been interrupted by a listing of names repeated twice:

> Boris, Roman, Olga, Mikhail, Anna, Larisa.
> Boris, Roman, Olga, Mikhail, Anna, Larisa.

The hypnotherapist and his wife had since given these names to the local strays that they fed and footed veterinary bills for.

He said that he had even developed remote comradery with other listeners. While in Athens last September for an annual international hypnotherapy conference, he met another with whom he had corresponded for over ten years—a mostly mute man, a lifelong bachelor and bellhop at the Hotel Grande Bretagne who tuned in during his work shifts via Zenith transistor and in the evenings on his home system. On his day off, a Tuesday, they met at a café in Exarchia and listened together over retsina and tiropita for an hour before parting ways. This man had the second-highest log rate, at eleven contributions. He had dedicated the past eighteen years of his life to listening.

The connection failed, and the hypnotherapist was fixed on the screen, distorted, eyes shut, mouth wide open—a black ovular portal set into his face as if leading to who knows where. He appeared to be calling out to me—or shouting.

The unintentional image looked like one of the Francis Bacon screaming-pope paintings, and I thought of the interview I'd read where Bacon says, *We nearly always live through screens—a screened existence. And I sometimes think when people say my work is violent that from time to time I have been able to clear away one or two of the veils or screens.*

I looked at the hypnotherapist, still frozen, and thought that perhaps this poor connection had cleared away a veil or two.

When we reconnected, his wife stood behind him—headless. He explained that his wife's studio router had a stronger connection. She told him to try this password: *pinturas negras*, all lowercase, replace the *s* in *negras* with a dollar sign and then the number 1, and then *Bolinas*, capital *B*, and then an exclamation point . . .

She went on to say that while she knew it to be

understood universally (by artists at least) as gauche to linger on the subject of Goya's *Pinturas Negras*, she did it anyway and, as long as I was made aware that she knew it was Klischeeanstalt, then she could speak freely of her long-standing attraction to, obsession with even, one painting in particular, *that one of the dog*.

She held a small print up to the screen—she had collected postcards and other reproductions of this painting, including a can of Goya black beans but over *beans* it said *paintings* and instead of the image of the beans was a haphazard rendering of the dog. Whenever she found herself blocked, she would paint her own. Why? Because, she said, it was the perfect representation of fear.

The hypnotherapist said to not get his wife started on the breed—there had been perennial debate over whether the dog depicted was a Chinese crested or a terrier mix—he was staunchly team crested.

The wife explained that her fixation with the painting began when her first husband, now dead, was making a documentary on the prison in Carabanchel, the southwestern suburb of Madrid. The documentary was not on the political tensions that arose around the prison but on the structure itself, a panopticon, which had been constructed by hostages during the Spanish Civil War. While her then husband was off shooting each day, she had many empty hours to walk through the dull suburb. It was so hot, she recounted. She explained that what she did not know then was that, when you have no particular place to be, and you are in a foreign or unfamiliar place, you are actually moving around with the specific purpose of locating a place within yourself at which you may or may not arrive.

On the third empty day, she had discovered, by the bank of the Manzanares, a small graffitied plaque marking the site of Quinta del Sordo, "House of the Deaf Man," a villa Goya had purchased from another deaf man. Goya himself had lost his hearing years prior after a sudden, acute illness. It was on the walls of this house that Goya had painted the fourteen paintings. No one was meant to see them. They were transferred from the walls onto canvas years after his death. Obviously, they are in the Prado now, she said. Where else would they be.

She explained that Goya abandoned Quinta del Sordo . . . With wistfulness in her voice she quoted the artist himself: *Who cannot extinguish the fire in his house should move away from it.* He wrote that shortly before going away. *This seems obvious but it's not . . .* she said. *Nothing is obvious to humans. Nothing at all. We willingly sit in fire . . .* She walked off the screen having delivered her lines.

We returned to the session. Unfixed, the hypnotherapist began.

He told me to let myself notice subtle changes in sounds from moment to moment.

> It doesn't really matter whether you go into trance sooner or later, he said. He told me to notice my hands, the way my body made contact with the cushions. To feel the heaviness as my body rested. It's nice to feel something familiar as you learn something new, he said. Become aware of the parts of your body being supported by the chair. And how the chair is supported by the floor and the floor is supported by walls and beams, and beneath this floor there are other floors that go deeper and deeper and deeper. That's right. It became apparent then that he was battling the emergence of a hiccup attack. Let your mind drift to any vista that captures your imagination. We learn things in an unusual way, a way that we do not know about. Scan your body.

He asked me, as I sank even farther into the chair, to recall an early memory of total liberation. Shut your eyes, he said, and feel each side of the lid and then feel the lid become a shield . . .

There was a visit to the San Diego Zoo's aviary. Age eight or nine . . . Around this time I had a particular interest in the birds of Egypt, after playing the minor role of the ornithologist in a primary school production of a theatrical adaptation of Oscar Wilde's *The Happy Prince* (a story about the friendship between a statue of the dead prince and a sad swallow whose flock flew off to Cairo and left him behind).

The aviary was built in the 1920s by a local architect and at the time was the most impressive of its kind in the world—a great vaulted structure, netting draped like skin over bone, fixed into the edge of a canyon to simulate a rookery. The structure was referred to as the "invisible cage"—assuming the bird's perspective. Inside were over one hundred birds, manmade brooks, channels, waterfalls, and artificial rain that let down once an hour on the hour, a feature added in the early 1990s.

Inside the cage, the birds were at first more difficult to see than I had hoped. I did not spot many but could sense their proximity. The green walls. I remember the air of freedom I felt within this enclosure too as I, alone, crossed elevated walkways over small brooks and canals beneath a tight green canopy. I had never felt so far away, as a true hot wind blew through the enclosure.

At once, the birds fell quiet and many lined up in

a great row along the only structural wire that ran through the center of the cage. I thought of the Rockettes. I assumed the birds were trained, performing some choreography or operating on a schedule. Their quiet procession went on for several minutes. The only sound remaining was that of the water coursing in all of its directions. Then, as though a switch had gone off, the birds resumed their singing and calling and once again disappeared.

When I left the aviary, which let out directly into the zoo's gift shop, I found a shopkeeper sweeping up many small mountains of broken glass within one giant puddle. She apologized for the shop's appearance. The entire wall of snow globes had come down off the shelf. Had I felt it? There had been an earthquake, 5.2 . . .

And when I opened my eyes, the hypnotherapist's own eyes were closed, his head tilted back, two floating hands holding his ears and nose shut. His own hand tilted water into his open mouth.

That night, unable to sleep, I read a post by Quicksand53 on a forum about Sudden Deafness that said birdsong was often the first thing to go. Quicksand53 had thought the birds no longer fancied the tree outside her kitchen window. Birds, like people, move on. But this was not the case, she realized, after making eye contact with a bird as she placed a cup in the sink. The whole flock was still in the tree singing, but her ears refused the song. Loss is a process, she said, not a light switch. Quicksand53 ended the post with, Good luck! followed by a link to a white noise machine with adjustable frequencies.

I fell asleep to The Buzzer, taking comfort in knowing that what most listeners were hearing was just this—not much—and that they too were waiting for words to erupt from the waves like little bombs.

The apartment above mine had a minor flood and a leak came down through the ceiling, right over the bed. I woke, face wet, and thought that I had been crying in my sleep. This was before I discovered my pillow was soaked through, before I noticed the hairline crack overhead. My emotional ceiling. I wiped my face dry and contacted the super. Can it wait till tomorrow? he asked.

When the super came to attend to the leak the next morning, he told me there was a new tenant upstairs. The jump roper had left and had been replaced by the former Miss Baltic Sea. And as the ceiling continued to let out over the bed, I came to think it was not a person but instead an ocean that had moved in above me. And I thought, People might look at this ocean and say, Oh, this ocean used to be so beautiful. Time is cruel even to oceans. What is this ocean doing in a fifth-floor walk-up?

Poor thing. Moving water is better than still water, said the super as he left again to find a wrench.

The following day, I saw Miss Baltic Sea in the entryway, and she was not blue and horizontal—she was blond and vertical, and unable to remove her mail key from her mailbox. I offered to help but she only smiled and threw the weight of her whole body in the opposite direction of the little key.

It was just before Christmas. The filmmaker requested we get one last dinner before his departure. We ate at an Italian place that serves crudités on cubes of ice, a place we had once frequented. Two patrons were on oxygen and the check came with two peppermints. He walked me home and came upstairs without invitation. On our way up, we passed the super carrying large paint buckets. The floor of the basement was repainted white every other Sunday—a by-product of an acute obsessive-compulsive affliction. When we got inside the apartment, the filmmaker said the super looked just like the actor who played Nazerman in *The Pawnbroker*—like Nazerman, the super was suspicious of everyone. Unlike Nazerman, the super was Sicilian from Staten Island, an ex-firefighter, a divorcé.

The filmmaker, who always had many factoids on hand, said that Quincy Jones composed the soundtrack for the film. The bossa nova used in the famous scene at a nightclub would later be used as the main theme to the *Austin Powers* film series. My hearing had lost its low end, and the filmmaker's voice sounded like the Chipmunks' or as though he'd sucked helium from a party balloon.

I only had water to offer him and he lay on the floor and asked me several questions in a row. His body was the hypotenuse cutting the room into two right triangles. When I told him that I had a sense that I was haunting myself, he said that he did not think that was possible. He said he actually believed he was haunted by someone who hadn't yet been born. One must be haunted by something from the outside in, he said. I disagreed.

By this point, the filmmaker already had a redheaded girlfriend waiting for him in California. She had moved ahead of him for a medium-sized acting job. And when he spoke about her, he spoke as if love were something you could hold against someone.

With love, he said, it's like people who build submarines. It's very specific. Nontransferable. The man who builds the switch must also switch the switch. And so you get stuck operating this one switch. Or not even operating it, just making sure you guard the switch so that no one else switches it.

Love, he said, is obviously a form of haunting. It's

a ghost sitting at the edge of the bed, the bed being, you know, the heart. And sometimes it requires an exorcist.

I had not realized until then that he was holding my foot in his hand. I told him I found him to be *un-haunt-able*, uninhabitable even for ghosts. He seemed offended. What I did not tell him was that he was actually like a termite that finds its way inside the walls of a house. And the termite, like a perfect houseguest, has a sense when it's stayed just long enough. Just long enough to have pushed the house to its absolute brink. Then it goes and leaves the house empty, eroded. I had once loved him.

That night, he had a look of impotence. A rented smile. A rented desire.

You should think of your illness as a play but *not* a film, he said. A play in which you are the spectator, the actor, and the critic at once. Eventually, you can be free from language. Spoken language is just form, not force. When doing mise-en-scène, we ask, What is everything that can be said independently of speech? The answer is anything that can be affected or disintegrated by it. Mise-en-scène is pure theatrical language. That's how you can live your life. That's how you can live your life if you want to.

Well that's not life, I said. He sat up then. No longer a hypotenuse but now a tangent. See, you can do something like this instead, he said. He kissed me then, and I let it go on until there was no way to determine who was kissing who.

It was minutes later, with my back against the wall, and the filmmaker's head between my legs, that I made perfect eye contact with the woman with the fanatical tick, and it struck me then that she had probably seen me as many times as I had seen her but that we had never seen each other at the same time. And I felt, in this moment of collision, like I was touching myself with no hands. Like the filmmaker had disappeared altogether. And in that instant, a dormant memory surfaced and replayed itself:

There had been a group decision made among several students, before an eighth-grade history class. (We were learning about Germany.) It had been decided that each boy was to stimulate the girl to his right. No one had ever stimulated or been stimulated before. The day before, we had watched the first hour of Fritz Lang's *Metropolis*, and the second half of the film was going to be screened the next class. (The teacher, a small man with a Sunkist beard, was not interested in teaching and often played films for the duration of our meetings.) We sat around the table and self-organized: boy, girl, boy, girl. And at one far end of the table was the paused screen.

We resumed at the scene in which the worker's city floods and children rush to the city center, pushing through the water like Chincoteague ponies, soundtracked by Wagner-imitation music, when I felt the button of my pants flick open and the zipper click its way down like a roller coaster moving to the top of its track. The children pile onto what looks like a Malevich sculpture as the water rises up around them. They become an island of young flailing bodies like the little fish in Bruegel's *Big Fish Eat Little Fish*. The dry finger that went into me belonged to a boy whom I'm told has since taken a position with the CIA. He had long unclipped nails. There was a ticklish girl, now a tax lawyer, who failed to contain her laughter. The teacher sensed a lack of attention and paused the film to tell us that for this scene, five hundred children from the poorest districts of Berlin had to work for fourteen days in a pool of water that Lang intentionally kept at a low temperature. The future CIA agent kept his hand in my pants and I had that feeling, like I was touching myself with no hands. After the class, he tried to kiss me and I politely declined but said, Thank you.

And it became obvious in this moment that the filmmaker still loved me, that I had misunderstood his love as pity. The longer he remained between my legs, the farther away from him I felt. As though my head were one hundred miles from where my body sat. I was thinking about Hanne Darboven again, about something a minimalist artist friend said just after she died: *She was in the process of building her own personal world. The only world ever created for her.*

I had this funny feeling like I was sitting in a puddle of liquid. Like my water had just broken. Like I was about to give birth and the filmmaker's head was in the way. And I realized that his water glass had emptied on its side. I, in turn, decided it was time and proceeded to fake an orgasm.

The next day, the hypnotherapist was all hard edges. A shadow had surgically cut his face into two. Half-moon biscuit. I began to speak and he shushed me, picked me up, and carried me over to the window. Can you hear them? he asked. But I could hear only his breathing. A heavy nose breath. It's the chimes of Paolo Soleri, he said, my Cosanti bells . . . The wind is blowing east! When the wind blows east, he explained, the tree sings. All I could see through the computer screen was a soft grid, the screen of his window. He told me that Cosanti was the combination of the Italian words *cosa* ("things") and *anti* ("against"). He told me that the first weekend of every September, he and his wife always drive to Paradise Valley, Arizona, to pick out a new bell for their Aleppo pine, from which hang thirty-two bells. In high winds, especially those coming off the Pacific, the sound of the tree can be overbearing. This is all part of it, he said. He told me that decades ago now, the summer after completing his first and only year of architecture school, he had volunteered at Cosanti. There he had apprenticed under the lead bell maker, another Italian who had a way with bronze.

And I told him that it was funny he mentioned architecture—it was during those weeks of increased dosage that I had felt an expanding sense of regret. A regret like water placed in a glass and then into a freezer—a feeling that grows hard and cracks everything around it. An oceanic regret that proved to me, only in that specific moment, that I had never actually felt regret before.

I told him that I had regretted not becoming an architect, that I had come from a long line of people who carry this regret, including my veterinarian mother, who lived with two architects while attending veterinary school and questioned her choice as she learned to express the anal glands of house pets. This regret had cycled in me. I had convinced myself that I wanted people to entrust me with their floors, their walls, their ceilings.

Illness, injury . . . are forms of castration, he said. It makes sense that you would have a desire to erect, so to speak. Anyway, he was not surprised—many architects are composers or musicians or wish they were and vice versa. It's obvious, he said, music is the architecture of sound. I told him that it felt like I spent most of my time interviewing myself. Each day was a long interview that seemed to carry on even in my sleep. He said that this was good, that it would help me become aware of a fuller spectrum of existence.

His wife—this time an extended black blur—walked past but did not stop by the screen. She was busy working on a writing project. Not enough hours in the day. She had taken a step back from painting. Instead she was working on something concentrated and durational—for the period of one month. A limitation was what she needed. The hypnotherapist explained that she was writing a romance novel—a romance with the self. But she would like it to be read as a painting.

He told me he would begin the session by reading out a quotation from D & G related to the way sound and refrain moves into the visual. Not Dolce and Gabbana!—Deleuze and Guattari . . . French not Italian . . . Philosophy not fashion . . .

> A bird found in the rainforest sings a complex song made up from its own notes and, at intervals, those of other birds that it imitates; it is a complete artist. This is not a synesthesia of the flesh but blocs of sensation in the

territory—colors, postures, and sounds that sketch out a total work of art. These sonorous blocks are refrains; but there are also refrains of posture and color, and postures and colors are always being introduced into refrains: bowing low, straightening up, dancing in a circle and a line of colors. The whole of the refrain is the being of sensation. Monuments are refrains . . .

The whole of the refrain is the being of sensation.
The whole of the refrain is the being of sensation.
The whole of the refrain is the being of sensation.

He repeated this sentence many times, and the more I thought about it, the less I understood it.

The whole of the refrain is the being of sensation.
The whole of the refrain is the being of sensation.
The whole of the refrain is the being of sensation.

The hypnotherapist's wife moved back and forth across the screen several times in quick black blurs— the opposite of a ghost.

He told me again to let myself notice subtle changes in sounds from moment to moment.

He told me to notice my hands, the way my body made contact with the cushions. He told me to feel the heaviness as my body rested. He told me it is nice to feel something familiar as you learn something new. *Become aware of the parts of your body being supported by the chair. And how the chair is supported by the floor and the floor is supported by walls and beams, and beneath this floor there are other floors that go deeper and deeper. That's right* . . . And then he began to tell a story about searching . . . The husband dug through the garbage underneath the kitchen sink. He was searching. He was searching for something unaccounted for. A steak. Where had it gone? . . . And I can't remember the rest of this story because I entered the intended state.

After the session, I walked the little black dog along her usual route. We followed the rats. In the hallway I passed my downstairs neighbor going through her mail wearing large sunglasses. When I asked her where she was spending the holidays, she said that Jesus was born in September and that Christmas is an opiate for the masses. That she didn't do opiates and didn't do the masses. She said that she liked May Day. Pagan fertility rituals. Poles. Posies. May 1 had always been one of her days. She seemed down.

That night, it arrived in the news that some American government employees stationed in Havana, Cuba, had heard an unfamiliar high-pitched sound and soon after began experiencing dizziness, nausea, and insomnia. That they could no longer think the way they had before hearing the sound. That some had experienced sudden hearing loss. It was suspected to be a case of mass hysteria, but the doctors who performed examinations after the episode found damage to the inner ear that was identical in each patient. There was an official statement by a doctor from Miami who said simply, These people have been injured and we are not sure how.

The statement said that the diplomats and officers were in their homes or hotel rooms when they were struck by a noise followed by the sensation of pressure to the head, and that officials unintentionally extended their exposure to the sound by walking around in search of its origin. When they opened their front doors, the sound was gone.

In the report, it was noted that these sound attacks had happened between ten and fourteen months prior to this reporting—old news—and I realized that I had been in Havana during the time in which the attacks had occurred. I had stayed in a casa particular in Vedado just off the Malecón, only blocks away from where many of the injured government officials were housed. The trip was short, just three days, to visit a friend who, at the time, was working at Taller Experimental de Gráfica, the oldest printmaking facility in Cuba.

On my first day there, my friend took me to the National Museum to see the work of Belkis Ayon, a Cuban printmaker who worked almost exclusively in gradients of black, white, and gray. Her work focused on rituals and imagery from Abakuá, an Afro-Cuban secret religious fraternity. The prints often contain figures that have large eyes and no mouths or ears. At twenty-six, Ayon was selected to represent Cuba in the Venice Biennale (she and her father rode their bikes to the airport with the art). By thirty-two, Ayon had shot herself in the head with her father's gun.

That night after a late dinner, we walked through Old Havana and ate turrón de coco in San Francisco Square. A very young boy tried to sell me claves. I had never been to Spain but I told her this was how I had pictured it—the architecture. We stopped into Basilica Menor de San Francisco de Asís, a Franciscan convent built in the 1500s. An esteemed Costa Rican pianist, Leonardo Gell, happened to be giving a recital. As the music began, a colony of bats appeared in great numbers and began to circle above the player. Members of the clergy flocked from the wings of the arches waving brooms and mops. One clergyman lost his toupee. The player stopped playing and sat with his hands on his lap. He shook his head and ran his hand back and forth through his black hair. He pulled up his sleeve and looked at his watch. The player and the audience sat in silence. All that could be heard was the hum of the bats as they moved through the air and occasionally a slap—when a mop met a bat. Finally, a very small man with a mop in a black cloak shouted, Lo sentimos. Hay una infestación. The player exited the stage.

I spent the second day in the casa particular with food poisoning. Curtains drawn. On the third day, we drove an hour outside of the city to a beach famous for beach glass. At the edge of the beach was a trifecta of abandoned Soviet high-rises. On the beach there was no beach glass. A black cloud appeared on the horizon and we swam in the water until the storm became impossible to ignore. My friend had come to Cuba to spread her father's ashes and never left. As we swam, she told me this was where she had spread them, Santa Maria del Mar. The rain was heavy by the time we made it back to the car. White lines of lightning met the metal posts that marked the lots of the sugarcane fields along the highway. I returned to New York City early the next morning.

I stopped reading the news. I called the friend in Thessaloniki and got her voicemail. I called another friend who I rarely talk to but always answers and got his voicemail. I called the filmmaker and got his too. I called my mother and got hers. I feared momentarily that I was the only person alive, but I could smell someone panfrying a steak. As I shut off the lights, I realized that I spent most of my time looking through the space that divided the kitchen area from the living area. That I was living most of my life within this one small, particular frame. I stood at the window and thought of the Queneau line: "The roofs of Paris, lying on their backs with their little paws in the air."

On The Forum, MusicMan58 noted:
In deafness, life is . . . implicit.

The next session took place early in the New Year. The hypnotherapist arrived in his frame dripping wet. The light was flat and his face inconclusive. He began without small talk and asked that I focus on one thing in the room only. He told me to transfer myself onto that thing. He asked that I become that thing, wherever it was. Be *over there*, he said, pointing nowhere. He set a timer and exited the frame.

I looked at something in his room, not mine. A small black painting hung in the top left corner of the screen.

I remembered reading about a color-field painter who spoke about one patch of red being less red than a wall of red. I thought then of how one moment of quiet was less quiet than a long stretch of it. But I found that this long stretch of quiet had in turn begun to feel louder than anything I had heard before.

The image had frozen without my knowledge and when he returned to the screen, he was completely dry and asking me how long the connection had been cut for.

He said this exercise was called The Portrait. He asked me if I had been able to successfully transfer myself onto anything in the room—this would allow me to make a portrait of myself as a ready-made object.

I told him no but that I would try it again in the future. He said he was just here to supply the tools and asked what object I had selected. I told him I had chosen the painting in the top left corner of the screen. He said in the future I should not choose art as the object of my portrait, and he apologized for not saying this in advance.

He said that the painting was painted by a painter who was known not for his paintings but for his frames. That this frame was not even made by the painter known for his frames but by a framer in the garment district. This painting was not known for anything besides its hanging right where it was. It was a gift from a friend who had received it by way of the dead—and had arrived in the mail, accompanied by a printed email that said, "The flowers are chrysanthemums."

He said that his wife liked it more than he did. He thought it was a nice painting but that yes, he was also suspicious of still lifes with black backdrops and unnatural light sources. Oil on canvas, 1970 or something. He said this painter had framed da Vinci's portrait of Ginevra de' Benci, Giotto's *The Epiphany*, and some Klines and Motherwells. He held a postcard with a reproduction of da Vinci's portrait in the frame. He said Léger was the framer's mentor when he was in Paris on the GI Bill and told him to give up painting. On CBS *Sunday Morning*, the correspondent said that the name of this painter of the chrysanthemums in the white vase was *like Kleenex in the framing world, a standard.*

He removed the painting from the wall and held it up to the screen. Here, he said. The flowers were painted like film stills, not photographs. That they had ongoingness. One red, one not red, another red, another white, and two more that were neither white nor red. What he loved about the painting was that it was painted as though it were getting dark, as though the light had just died in the room of the painting, and minutes later the flowers would be invisible. He said there once was a landscape architect who said: They are actually peonies.

He told me, as he stepped away from the screen, that an email had just arrived from the listener in Athens, who had sent him a photograph from the roof of the Hotel Grande Bretagne, of the super-moon rising over the Acropolis.

I told him that the night before, a singer had fallen to her death in Athens climbing to her roof to see the same moon. The moon, so full of itself, doing what it is known for, he said. So today the flowers are for the singer, he said as he placed the painting back onto the wall. I told him that this singer reminded me of Ginevra de' Benci—short red curls, fair, Florentine, gone. When a life ends it's like a frame, he said, telling you exactly where to look, to see a thing complete as art. Some days we are less of ourselves. Some days we are portraits in reverse.

By the second week of the New Year, I had received only one message from the filmmaker since he had arrived in Los Angeles: a photograph of his new kitchen—on the stove was the stainless steel kettle I had given him three or four birthdays ago. The red-headed girl's back was turned as she removed something from the fridge. It was followed by the short text, *you made an appearance in my last dream . . .* I chose not to reply.

There are people who lie about their dreams. They make them up as they go. They give themselves permission. They feel a sudden need to entertain, to say something without any discernible meaning, maybe something shocking or maybe something subtle where nothing much happens. Then there are a subset of these people who lie about having had dreams featuring you or about you. This is usually performed by those who want to get in touch but have no reason to. They are too scared to say, I thought of you. Everyone does this at some point or another, I think—I did it once and it felt very strange. A dream is an unprovable lie . . .

I rarely dream, and if I do, I don't remember having dreamed. The last thing I remember dreaming was shouting, Pray for me, and someone shouting back, Pray for yourself! I have never prayed. But see, this could be a lie too . . .

It snowed, then it rained. God is always undoing something. The friend in Thessaloniki called as I was getting into the shower to tell me she had met someone new. An anarchist. Their sex was the best she had ever had but he did not approve of her online-shopping addiction or the fact that she was receiving funding from the Greek government. He walked in the door and she had to get off before I could say one word.

I once again returned to The Forum, where I counted five members who noted hearing the same phantom sound—the song "Silent Night":

> Hi from the finger lakes. Severe hearing loss, started with Silent Night. Female. Sounds like all male choir. Excellent choir. I can make them change songs.

> I hear Amazing Grace and Silent Night. Sometimes I hear old time country music. It was so bad at my sister's house that I went downstairs to sleep on the couch. It stopped. Now why?

> It's not the national anthem, Silent Night or Handel's Messiah anymore—just a constant sound like a lot of bees. My problem is that it interferes with my ability to listen to real music like at a concert, on TV, CDs, etc. The real music is distorted and so out of tune that I can barely recognize what I am hearing.

Hello! 18f. Moderate Loss left ear and right. I hear metal music playing when the moving fan in my room faces my direction. If fan is on rotate/low setting I hear Silent Night . . . which reminds me of church and no offense but I hate church.

It started with a brass band version of Battle Hymn of the Republic and I now get several others, Silent Night often, but can usually manipulate them to change when they get to me . . .

Lately, I had been spending my evenings listening to music that I did not want to forget. I believed that the more I listened to these songs, the more clearly I would be able to replay them for myself in a future when I could no longer hear them. I limited what I listened to, worrying there might be a limit to what I could retain with specificity.

But soon I found myself bored by the slim selection and the repetition and feared that this process of sonic tattooing might ruin the music itself. I no longer associated the songs with memories but rather the songs themselves became memories. I stopped listening to music altogether. The highest-fidelity sound is in the head.

For a portion of our final session, the hypnotherapist read aloud a story from his book of Ericksonian
Hypnosis about a young woman, my age, who, while
walking through a Northern Italian town, comes
upon a boiler factory. He asked that I close my eyes
and began:

> The crews work on twelve boilers at the
> same time and there are three shifts of
> workmen that work around the clock.
> Those pneumatic hammers were pound-
> ing away, driving rivets into the boilers.
> She heard the noise and she wanted to
> find out what it was. She went inside and
> she couldn't hear anybody talking. She
> could see the various employees were
> conversing, and she could see the fore-
> man's lips moving, but she couldn't hear
> what they said. The foreman heard what
> she said. She asked him to come outside
> so she could talk to him and then she
> asked him for permission to roll out her
> blanket and sleep on the floor for one
> night. He thought there was something
> wrong with her. She explained that she
> was a premedical student and that she

was interested in learning processes and he agreed. He explained to the crew and left a note for the next shift. In the morning, when she awoke, she could hear the workmen talking about that damn fool girl. What in the hell was she sleeping on the floor there for? What did she think she could learn?

And as he read from the book, I sat with my eyes still shut but found my face had become caught up in a dogged smile—so obstinate that any attempt to drag down the corners of my mouth would make them go the other way. The pull of this particular smile felt like an attempt at dragging two dogs for a walk in the rain, their homes being in opposite directions. I began to laugh and felt embarrassed, worried I would offend him. There was nothing funny about the story, other than its lack of effect. There was the hopelessness of my situation. The innocuous story. Then the sadness I felt gave way to laughter.

He continued:

During her sleep that night, she was able to blot out all that horrible noise of the twelve pneumatic hammers and she could hear voices, the voices in the factory.

And then he continued reading but it was as though he was addressing me:

> You have roaring in your ears but you haven't thought of tuning them so you don't hear the roaring. And you think back. There are a godly number of times this morning, this afternoon when you don't hear the buzzing. It is hard to remember things that don't occur. The ringing did stop but because there was nothing there, you don't remember it. Now the important thing is to forget about the ringing and remember the time there was no ringing. She learned in one night's time not to hear the pneumatic hammers and to hear the conversation she could not hear the previous day . . .

I thought, as he read on, of the twin scenes from *The Story of Adele H* starring Isabelle Adjani. Adele has followed her ex-lover from Paris to Halifax in an attempt to recover her heart. In Halifax, she attends a hypnosis, performed at a small local theater. A row of candles line the edge of the wooden stage. As the hypnotist prepares to bring his subject, a young woman, into her state, he tells her, It's all right now, you can relax, everything is fine now. He has a radio voice, a pencil mustache, and a face glinting with sweat.

The woman lies back on a wooden platform at the center—it all appears very surgical. He will open her right up. As the hypnotist leans over her small body, he tells her again, Everything is fine now, everything, everything, everything. And just then, as she slips off, an audience member, a man in a red municipal police coat, stands up and starts to walk out of his row, shouting—It's just a big fake, it's all a fake, it's a fake. He tells the hypnotist to get off the stage. And the hypnotist says if he is so clever he should come down there. The hypnotist takes the woman out of her state of hypnosis as the heckler climbs down the risers. The hypnotist says that when he counts to three, she will be awake. One, two, three. She opens her eyes as if for the first time and takes a bow. Then comes the applause and she disappears. The hypnotist turns to the impassioned man in red, who is now on the stage. The hypnotist tells the impassioned man in red to make himself at home. He tells him he will have to put him to sleep since he's so willing. He asks him to remove his hat and to just forget about everything, to listen carefully, to concentrate, to follow every one of the orders.

You're *very tired*, *very* tired. Your hands, your arms are very heavy, your legs are heavy like lead.

Within a few moments you will fall into a deep sleep and now at one your eyes are falling heavily down, at two your eyes are closed, at three you are fast asleep. It's a beautiful day and you are rowing on a beautiful lake . . . It's very hot, I mean *very* hot.

The man in red begins to row and row, his eyes are shut and he appears to be breaking a sweat . . . It's very hot, and he's rowing hard. Harder, harder, you've got a long way to go. It's very hot out, you can unbutton your coat. Now you are rowing very hard. Good. Good. Harder and harder and harder now. Now you can undo your trousers. The hypnotist turns to the audience and says that if he wanted to, he could force this man to leave the police and finish his life in a monastery—but, he says, we aren't going to go that far today. That's enough. When he counts to two, he will wake up and go away—one, two, and the man's eyes flash open and he flies off the stage and out of the theater half-dressed. The audience goes wild.

After the show, Adele finds her way backstage—she tells the hypnotist how impressed she was with his work but that she was not just there to tell him that. As he removes his pencil mustache in the mirror with white cream, she tells him how intrigued she is by his power. But he is simply an instrument of force, he says. She tells him she would like to hire him for a personal matter. Could he change someone's feelings? He asks for an example. Love to hate, or vice versa. He is sorry but he can only work on bodies not souls. (And to myself, I think, This is true for any doctor.) All he can do is force certain people to act against their wills. She suggests instead of love, a marriage. That would be possible, but it would require two witnesses and a minister—not easy but not impossible, just a matter of money. As they discuss payment, the man in red who had run off naked enters the dressing room, now clothed, holding the folded red uniform, hat, and badge. He asks the hypnotist where he'd like him to put his costume for the next performance.

And as I watched the hypnotherapist talk, I imagined removing my clothes at the end of our session. Folding my costume, my blue sweater, and passing it back through the screen, returning it to him for the next show.

How do you feel now? he asked, after telling me to open my eyes, which were already open. I told him that today was a clearer day, and that on clearer days, when the inflammation was down, when my voice had quieted and others had loudened again, I felt that dread of verifiable happiness—the full-body anticipation of its departure. Even the slightest wind could carry it away . . .

He said that while this was a palliative care trial, this was not *just* palliative care—that helplessness could give way to wonderful things, that helplessness looked like a very large net with very large holes and that I must be willing to trail that net in the sea for some time before lifting it out to see what I had caught. Of course, there is the sense that any progressive illness moves faster than time. Outpacing it, leaving the days panting, trying to catch up. I explained my sense that the clock was intensely ticking. And he told me to stop imposing my own feelings onto the clock's ticks. And just like that, we were out of time.

Later, on The Forum, a twenty-year-old woman wrote about her fear of sex, the concern that she might sound like a donkey or worse, a monster. What really bothered her, she said, was that even when people let themselves go they have some degree of inhibition, which would not be possible for her—she would not know what she would have to inhibit. Another woman suggested that if she wasn't sure how loud she was when she came, she might consider setting up a computer or phone to record the sound as she *took care* of herself—this would show the decibels. She would then know if the sound was as bad as she feared. If it showed she was loud, she could practice making herself quieter. In the same thread, two men discussed the pros and cons of visiting bars and going clubbing around Gallaudet, a university for the deaf. One said, You can say all sorts of things you've always wanted to say in the sheets.

THEN IT WAS the end of January—five months.

After the next hearing test, the specialist noted that while my decline was at first like an expert run on a mountain, it was now more intermediate, gentler. And I felt it, snowy, and blank before me—open, white, slowed. A light wind in my hair. A longer, wider run. I could take in my surroundings as I cruised downward. It was a more leisurely decline. I had never skied. The specialist said this was just another phase. He said it was typical. He said there was a new trial in east Los Angeles at a private institute specific to ears. The facility was shaped like a seashell, he said, just like the spiraled pathway of the cochlea. He said, Isn't that so Los Angeles?

I met the criteria. He said that I should try anything I could, that windows close and eventually become walls. He noted that she was a particularly beautiful woman, the doctor. He could say that because he was gay, he said. She looked like Jane Fonda.

I wrote to the filmmaker to tell him I was coming to Los Angeles and received an immediate reply insisting that I stay with him and the girlfriend. There was a second bedroom. I would stay part of the week. Two days of treatment. Two days of leisure. I left for California the following week.

When I landed at LAX, I received a message. The filmmaker would be gone for the night but the girlfriend would be there to pick me up in passenger-pickup Zone 4 in a bronze Subaru with racks on the roof. And when I stepped into the sunlight it hit me like a smile from a stranger that I was unable to return. And then there was the smile of the girlfriend, who called out my name like an old friend. Her hair was no longer red but blond. For a part. There was a roof box on top of the car that looked like an aerodynamic coffin.

On the dashboard were several rocks, one shell, a nail clipper, rose water. She asked immediately if I had interest in a yard sale. It was Sunday. There was a yard sale at the house of an aging Swedish pop star, a recent mother and divorcée, a friend of a friend's friend. It was on the way home. She asked my shoe size. Six and a half. She was a seven. And she had heard that the Swedish pop star was also a seven.

I was reminded of the phase of my childhood during which I had looked up, compulsively, the shoe sizes of celebrities. As we drove down a boulevard, the sky in front of us was cloudless and just one even shade of blue end to end like a backdrop for a school picture day.

The girlfriend said I was missing the blizzard in New York. I said I knew, that I loved snow. On the plane, with the engines going, I had thought about whether silence was translucent or opaque. My reasoning canceled itself out. I thought of the snow . . . When there is enough of anything, it becomes so deeply itself that you lose track of its ending. There are those moments on airplanes where the engine goes quieter or changes its rhythm and—we wait very patiently and expectantly in that instant to be dropped from the sky. I had this over Arizona.

On the 110, at a standstill in the South Figueroa corridor, she said how nice it was that I had remained such good friends with the filmmaker, that she couldn't continue loving someone she'd decided to stop loving. That the continuation of love is a skill. She asked me then if I still loved him. I could be honest, she said. Not exactly, I said. She told me that I had a beautiful body. That the filmmaker's old computer was now hers and that she had seen many photographs of me. She asked if I liked Los Angeles. I had her roll up the windows; I couldn't hear her at all.

I told her that Los Angeles gave me this feeling that I was perpetually on the edge of town. Never arriving. She liked that about LA, loved that about it actually. She said she was from the San Fernando Valley. She loved the heat. The kind of heat that feels like sitting under the exhaust pipe of a car after a hundred-mile-plus drive. She said she liked the kind of heat that could kill you. She told me that her mother was a nihilist and her father was an optimist. That he had died. She said she came from a long line of suicides on her mother's side and that her mother was the last of three sisters standing. She loved her life, she said. Things felt very easy for the first time. She felt this with the filmmaker. I said when something felt easy it often made me uneasy. There was traffic. She rolled the windows down again.

At the sale, the girlfriend was very focused on footwear. She said she had a thing for shoes, that her father had called her Imelda Marcos as a teenager. I overheard a man with many rings on his hands say to another man who was barefoot that the house was designed by Schindler in 1953. The house looked like a flat-roof international style from the street, but it was all shed and gable roofs on the garden-view side. As a result, the interior was a syncopation of ceiling heights and changing axes.

The girlfriend wanted my opinion because she said she trusted it. She held my hand and said we had such a similar sense of style. All of the shoes fit her and the Swedish pop star came up and said that her feet had grown by a half size when she gave birth, otherwise she wouldn't be getting rid of these. She had worn the pair on the girlfriend's feet for a show in Rotterdam. She held her son in her arms. The toddler glared at me and I smiled back. Then he looked content. The girlfriend turned to me and said she wanted children in the next two years and that, when she did, I could have her shoes.

There was another singer there who was known and loved by a specific circle of people only interested in their own specific circle—she was looking through the dresses one by one. I found her attractive. She reminded me of a version of myself I'd once thought was possible. The girlfriend said that the lesser-known singer didn't have friends but that a lot of people wanted to be her friend, that when she had begun hanging out with the Swedish pop star, she'd developed a certain mentality, even though she still can't afford a housekeeper. We stopped at a Cuban deli for small pastries filled with dulce de leche. She said that she was addicted to these things. We stopped for gas and I offered to pay. She accepted. She said she had to do a self-tape audition when we returned before making dinner.

As we drove on, the San Gabriel Mountains appeared flat against the horizon—like they belonged to painting, not sculpture. But as the light broke out into pieces, the mountains proved themselves. Off the freeway, the sun finally set, and our headlights caught every piece of kicked-up dust. It was as though each piece of dust desperately wanted a role in the Great Film by the Great Director. I felt I was looking at the discarded halos of the supposed angels of the city. And suddenly it was just dark. The sky, starless.

The apartment was on the second floor of a split-level Spanish-style house. It was all white inside with terra-cotta floors, no rugs, two daybeds, three books. The lamps all had pleated shades. I smelled jasmine. On the kitchen counter was a bottle of alcohol-free wine and several little blue tubes with dissolvable sugar pellets from the health food store. One for fever, one for depression, one for bruising, one for gas, one for stress, one for motion sickness, one for acid reflux, one for sleep. There were many different vinegars next to the stove where the kettle I had given the filmmaker sat. The girlfriend taped her monologue in the other room—it was something about a makeshift abortion, with a lot of tears.

That night, at the table, she said that she felt some guilt that the man she loved had love for me that wasn't resolved. That our love preceded theirs. She was interested in chronology—she respected it. I asked her what she meant and she said that the order in which things happen is important, as if I had suggested otherwise. She said that she was sorry I was going through what I was going through. I told her that it felt less like I was going through something and more like I had become the thing. She asked me how I could smile while I was talking about something so terrible. She said she once had to leave a silent retreat early, that she couldn't help but mouth words or whisper. Then she stood at the sink washing dishes. I watched her move her hips back and forth to music. I could only hear the faucet.

We ate brown rice with pickled vegetables— turnips, radishes, carrots, kohlrabi, onions—that the filmmaker had pickled prior to his departure. There was only one small light on in the whole house and the windows and doors were open. I said it seemed there were very few bugs in Los Angeles and she agreed. I asked her if she would please shut off the music that was playing quietly . . .

She asked me if my mother was from South America; she said that I didn't look entirely white. I told her that I was entirely white. She said my eyes were so far apart. She said she wanted to know me better and touched my hand. She said she understood why he had loved me. She said that she read his emails but it was okay, he knew that she did this. Her hand rested on top of mine while she spoke and eventually she started drawing figure eights with her pointer finger between my knuckles. I told her that I was falling asleep. For me, it was 3:00 a.m.

The spare room was not a room but rather a corner with a rattan divider and a piece of cloth that said O S A K A. She undressed and I could see as she faced the mirror that our chests were almost identical, down to the nipple. She said she was a boy until she was nine and that her father had said, You're not a boy you're a girl, and that was that. She shut off the light and disappeared and I could hear her shut the windows and I could hear her shut the door and I could hear her get on the phone with the filmmaker and I could hear myself fall asleep.

The next morning, on my way to the clinic, my older male driver told me that he was a second-generation Angelino. He came from a long line of dry cleaners on his father's side and restaurateurs on his mother's, both originally from Lebanon.

My hearing had dropped again and it sounded like he had sucked the helium from a party balloon. As we drove down Melrose and passed the gates of the Paramount lot, he said that there was so much more to this town than the movies, that he hated actors. You're not an actor, I can tell, he said. At the light, I remembered what my landlord had told me during my interview. I thought about my apartment sitting there on the lot covered in a cape of dust. I remembered the landlord saying it was fitting because she was someone who always had two of the things she liked, just in case. And in that moment I felt like a duplicate of myself, like I was thinking from inside my body in New York but that I had entered the body of a stunt double at the intersection of Melrose and Western. That I was, after all, an actor.

The driver said the Paramount entrance gates reminded him of the family home in Beirut that now belonged to his cousin—the best cardiologist in Lebanon. I asked what kind of restaurant his mother had. Fast-casual, he said. It's a long story that ends in death, he said. For a while we drove on in silence. The window was cracked, which made a sound like a blanket being shaken violently of sand. We got on the freeway. He said that he should have a house in Calabasas but that his cousin who had run the family business shot and killed his sister and his mother before killing himself. The deaths had divided the family, he said, impeding the growth of the business. He asked if I had been to Zankou Chicken. I had not. Good, don't go, he said. And again, we drove in silence until he left me at the building shaped like a shell, shaped like an ear.

Inside the institute, there were almost no patients and young men in white coats walked in and out of doors with a sense of importance. One of the young men received me from the waiting area and performed the intake. He delivered me to my first exam and in the testing booth, I found that the man's voice was the same as the one in the booth in New York and that he said the same four words: *baseball, hot dog, ice cream, airplane.* The words would eventually be dialed down to nothingness. But before that they became sounds I could sense but not hear. Like someone pursing their lips and releasing little gusts of air. I had to keep my hand raised until I could no longer hear a word and lower it when it disappeared. There was something comforting about the fact that this voice and these words had followed me to California.

I was reminded of two years before, when I had been working part-time for a video artist who one day asked me to find a voice actor who could imitate the female voice of the New York City MTA. I spent a morning looking at listings on local work-for-hire pages until I decided to look for the voice itself. There had been a recent human-interest piece on the woman behind the voice, in the *Bangor Daily News.* The woman lived in Maine with her husband, a

minister at their local church. She did her recordings
from their second bedroom. I searched the minister's
name and his nondenominational church appeared.
On the church's website was an online yellow pages
that listed the home numbers and addresses of the
members of the congregation. I looked up the address, which revealed the estimated value of their
home and a photograph of its exterior, plastic clap-
board, a young Japanese maple, and a maintained
front lawn. Without thinking, I dialed the number.
On the fifth ring I caught her, fixing lunch. I apologized immediately and felt the shame you feel when
walking in on a stranger using the toilet or changing in a dressing room. You found me, the voice said,
laughing in discomfort.

I told her I was very sorry to bother her but I was
calling to see if she had an agent I might be able to
speak to about hiring her to read some text for an art
installation. She said it was nice of me to ask but that
she didn't own her voice. She had sold it to a technology company, Innovative Electronic Designs, in
the early seventies. She was contractually prohibited
from speaking for anyone but them. She apologized,
saying she was an artist herself, that she would like
to help other artists but that she was also a woman
of her word and wouldn't do anything under the table. When I asked her what kind of art she made,
she said she was a singer. I asked what kind. Soul,

she said. She told me she hated her talking voice but loved her singing voice.

She told me that she had only ridden the subway once, in 1957, with her mother. That she didn't like tight spaces. She said that on the subway it was her voice that supplied the information, but the man gave the command to stand clear of the doors. Meanwhile she announced the transfers, the next stops, whether the trains were running express or local, uptown or downtown. I told her that I had imagined that they were a married couple, the two voices. No, she said, her husband was a minister. She told me she was also the voice of the Paris Metro; of departures and arrivals at Kennedy, O'Hare, and Newark; and of Typhoon Lagoon Water Park at Disney World. They had asked her to do a Disney-like voice, she said, very sexy and thoughtful and friendly.

I then recalled the time as a very young child when I had been stuck with my mother and a friend and her mother on It's a Small World, the water-based Stygian boat ride located in Fantasyland. It was the first and only time I was taken to an amusement park. The boat ran along a track in a tunnel home to three hundred mid-century audio-animatronic dolls singing the attraction's title song. We had entered the Polynesian territory, moved through a rainforest, and arrived in Hawaii, where dolls danced the hula surrounded by small rings of fire, when the boat failed to move down the river. The song repeated so many times that eventually it failed to register as a song.

I remembered arguing with my friend about who got to sit on the outermost seat on the boat, closest to the dolls. Eventually they cut the power and we sat in the tunnel in the type of darkness where you can't even see your own hands. And in the instant before children started shrieking came a moment of extreme quiet that only survives the initial prick of shock or fear.

The voice told me that she had begun her career as an administrator at a local radio station in Iowa where one day she filled in for a man who read out the weather forecast. She told me her voice is often asso-ciated with emergencies. She used to spend hours a day recording, she said, but now with technology they could make her say things she had never said and so they rarely called her. She told me she would rather be a voice that's faceless than a face that's voiceless.

I realized I had taken up a lot of this voice's time. It was nice to hear her voice, I told her. Yours too, she said. She laughed again. She asked that I stay in touch: voicegal2@*******.com. I wrote her a note thanking her for her time, to which she never replied.

In the booth, when I heard the familiar voice, I thought of her. Then, behind the glass, a physical man appeared and he read a series of words I was asked to repeat back to him:

Say the word *bluff*.
Say the word *goddess*.
Say the word *brink*.
Say the word *confess*.
Say the word *lick*.
Say the word *tan*.
Say the word *soil*.
Say the word *dote*.
Say the word *loss*.
Say the word *slim*.
Say the word *home*.
Say the word *tear*.
Say the word *loop*.
Say the word *help*.
Say the word *stint*.

He had nothing to say about my imagination . . . It was Los Angeles.

When I returned from the clinic it was dark and the filmmaker was there in the kitchen cooking with the girlfriend and I sat at the table watching them. No one spoke. It smelled of cardamom. The winds were high and the windows and doors were shut and the air in the room felt thin, like it was something passed between the three of us. The palms beat the glass like small dogs wanting to be let in. The film-maker said he got a nail in his tire.

As we ate, they faced me like an interview but only the girlfriend talked. She complained that it seemed all directors she hoped to work with were now only interested in casting nonactors. That suddenly authenticity was something impossible for an actor to have. That it was a phenomenon among directors right now. Her voice was low.

I told her that I felt like each person in my life had become a nonactor—that I thought of Bresson, who made his models do the same take so many times that they went beyond the take to arrive at something else. That words just flowed through them. Inflection escaped like air from a balloon. That that was how people's real selves came through. I told her that to me everyone's voice sounded the same now, that actually everyone's voice sounded like my own. Like a monochrome. Like the same take, over and over again. The filmmaker had put on music and I asked him to shut it off and he asked me what the music would do to me and left it on and the girlfriend said to turn it off and he looked at me and said it was okay with authority. He said we could only protect ourselves from so much.

A voice sang about parallelograms:

Paralelo-lelo-lelo-lelogram.
Spiralelo-lelo-gram.
Spiralelo-lelo-lelo-lelogram.

Quadrehedral.
Tetrahedral.
Mono-cyclo-cyber-cilia.

And I thought about the last time I'd seen him. The last time I had seen him, just before Christmas, when he had divided my home into two right triangles. Now he was talking and I was not listening. I was looking at him as if he were a photograph. My listening cut in again as he said he was going to butcher a quote—it was something like, It was a collision between predestination and free will, between chance and necessity. And then I was just watching again. I was willing myself not to hear a thing he was saying. I was not listening. I was just watching. I was practicing only watching. I was practicing how it would feel. I was practicing watching the girlfriend put food in her mouth and wipe vinegar off her lips. I was watching her laugh hysterically. And then so was the filmmaker. I was practicing watching the vinegar spill across the wood. I was practicing doing everything but listening. Then I said LA was too quiet for me. I stopped listening again. But I knew he was talking about the time we had visited a psychic in Santa Fe while visiting his father and his father's new wife. I was watching him talk. We had seen a psychic who told me that, by the end of my twenties, I would come across a body, and that I would have to confront that body. The girlfriend asked me to clarify. A dead body? I said that I didn't know. I let the words continue to roll over me. Swimming in the Rockaways, the filmmaker had told me that if I dove deep enough, the wave would not push me back. I thought, Is this acting? I was not listening but then I heard him say that he loved the part when passersby stared into nothingness. He said that it is the impression of a thing and not the thing itself that matters. Who is he? I thought. I had not been listening. He said, Why are you crying? She said, Are you okay?

Later, I was lying down on my back and they flanked me, talking across me. Their words passing over like little jets. And the filmmaker got up to make tea. And the girlfriend looked at me and said she wished her eyebrows were as dark as mine. She said that she was regrettably vain and so was her mother. Her hair was wet and had dripped onto her shirt in the shape of Florida. She went quiet. I felt then that when someone speaks to you it is like they're touching you. But then she did touch me. First, she leaned over me and for a second it looked like she had three eyes. Then she placed her lips on my lips and left them there for a moment. Like a conductor ordering an orchestra to rest—a fermata that lasts so long the audience goes home. I had been told by several people in my life that I had a habit of leaving glasses and other objects on the very edges of tables. One of the humble ways a death drive presents itself, someone once said to me. Then there was another shadow across the wall and then there was the touch of a third, familiar hand. Something searched me, as if for a ring down a drain. Something pushed me. Something kissed me. Something held me. Something left me. And I did feel then as though I had become the glass on the edge of a surface. That any movement at all could bring me to the floor. One by one, we each fell, quiet.

And much later, she blew out a candle and said good night like a mother or maybe like a daughter to a mother. I couldn't decide. The tea is still good cold, he said in the dark. A hand, his, tucked hair behind my ear and then went away. And I thought of that Lispector line from "Love": "Before going to bed, as if putting out a candle, she blew out the little flame of the day." What does it look like to let a day burn forever? Perhaps that's what it is to lose memory. To let a day burn to the wick and somehow then leap from the glass and burn all the things surrounding it—so it's no longer a little flame but a fire that spreads and takes up the objects of our past, present, and future.

The next morning, I returned to the great shell and I thought, I am a sea snail. That's all I thought. They took several vials of blood from me and lined them along the window and the sun shone through them and a nurse made a joke about Holy Communion and Jesus Christ that went over my head.

I returned to New York the following night.

IV

WHEN I ENTERED the apartment I thought I might find myself there. But the house was empty and just as I had left it and there was only one of me. I read once that a body is defined by duration, that a body in the present is inseparable from its previous state, linked in a continuous duration . . . and so on and so on . . . I felt in the present like I was living always alongside what a previous body had felt like. Perhaps this was why I had expected to find myself in the apartment when I returned home from California that night.

Later, in bed, I was jet-lagged and found myself

unable to sleep. My mother, like me, unable to sleep, sent over a text with a link: *Are you home? On view for one week only . . . A comet. Find a dark place.*

The following night, with nothing to do, I took the A Train to Beach 67. I had never been in winter. It was February—now dark by 5:20 p.m. It was just after 10:00 p.m. The express ran local. The night was see-through, black, unmoving; it just seemed to go on and on—the water, ironed flat. At the subway entrance, a wide woman wearing a headlamp sold mango and water from a red metal cart and she approached me before apologizing, first in Spanish and then in English. I was not who she thought I was; in fact, she thought I was her daughter. She is late! she told me. She laughed from inside her discomfort. This happens, I told her, referring to either the lateness or the mistaking. Even though she hadn't asked, I offered that I was there to get away from the city lights and to see the comet. Comet? No, she did not know this word. I asked my phone to translate. Cometa, I said. ¡Agujero brillante! she said. Cometa! She had never seen one but also she had never looked for one. She told me, Mi padre trabajaba en una fábrica que fabricaba piezas para telescopios. I could not understand her and had her type into my phone. She had, for this dying minute, blinded me with the bright hole at the center of her head.

I continued down to the beach where the ocean

had disappeared, as if a heavy curtain had been drawn across the shoreline. Edge to edge. I looked east along the beach at the lifeguard towers, which stood in the skirts of boardwalk lights. These lookout towers— unfinished thoughts repeating themselves—dotted the distance with small white deviations.

Living in a city, I rarely look up at the sky. I only do so when I am told to. That night in the Rockaways as I waited on the sand, I thought, So is this how comets advertise themselves? As one prolonged silence in the sky? A wet white star dragged across a black sheet? A mistake—touched before dried? I too am impatient, I thought . . . I remembered Woolf going on about the sky in "On Being Ill"—"One should not let this gigantic cinema play to a perpetually empty house." Tonight, I am the house, I thought. I saw the comet—a weak flashlight. God searching the basement.

Later that night, back home, in the news was a segment on comets. One piece featured the astronomer Johannes Kepler, the same astronomer whose name had emerged from the droning on The Buzzer, logged as an anomaly.

The cohost of the segment explained that Kepler had read about the dream of a great general who, on a dark night, in a high place, hears a very loud, very beautiful sound. In the dream the general is told it's just the planets, locked apart in gaps, that a sound is made as they move—*The moon emits the lowest, the heaven emits the highest . . . etc. The Earth, on the other hand, is stuck at the center of the universe . . .* And that later Kepler turned the dream into a fact. That he converted the changing speeds of planets into tones—the song of each planet, the product of the shape, size, and changing speed of each orbit. That it was one tune that was always quietly changing. That it was a great equation. And that he never heard the music. He said it was a continuous song for several voices, to be perceived by the intellect not the ear.

I thought of *Roland Barthes by Roland Barthes* when Roland Barthes says, "Je vois le langage." He calls it a disease—to see language—and likens it to this general's dream. "The primal scene, in which I listen without seeing, is followed by a perverse scene, in which I imagine seeing what I am hearing." I try to picture seeing what I am not hearing though I am unable to picture anything at all.

Attention in the news special was diverted to Kepler's mother, Katherina, who was eventually deemed a witch (I found I share a birthday with her only daughter, Margaretha). There were many pointing fingers. Katherina did time alone chained in a stone cylinder on the edge of town but was spared execution and freed because, by that point, her son was both a celebrity astronomer and a blind man. Both admired and pitied. Now there's a statue erected in her honor in their town on the very edge of the Black Forest, also famous for Kirschwasser—the clear, colorless brandy made from the double distillation of morello cherries—and the cuckoo clock.

Later on, in the news segment, they played an archival interview from the seventies with a geologist and a jazz pianist. Three hundred and fifty-four years after Kepler made the composition, the geologist and the pianist got in touch with a woman at Bell Labs to perform the piece for the ear. She was learning to program that era's giant computers. They had synthesized the music of the spheres using the calculations, notations, and theories of Kepler. "There's a great cosmic rhythm out there," the jazz pianist said. He recommended holding the speakers against your sternum for maximal vibration. For the next three hours I listened to the song of the planets, interrupted hourly by sponsorship messages from businesses and organizations. And as I listened, I lost track of my own machine. I could no longer tell if it was Pluto singing, Mars crying, Saturn humming, or my own blown fuse.

I held the radio to my sternum as it played on—knowing there was one sound in this suite that only I could transcribe—before doing the four days of dishes I had been avoiding. As I listened I confirmed for myself that I had found a well of emotion I hadn't known was there, like coming upon water in the middle of a desert—depression, the source itself—inexhaustible, sustaining, pitch. A drone droning.

I walked the little black dog. I prepared another white fish—this time with sage, lemon, and thyme—and while watching the oil heat in the pan, I could not decide whether I was more like a blind man looking up at the sky or an angry woman in a stone cylinder. Out the window: I looked up without being told to. The stars—little silences or shrapnel from the halos of angels.

In bed that night I heard a quiet constant rushing, a small waterfall. It was not Miss Baltic Sea but rather the shower, which I had left on accidentally and failed to hear until my head was propped against the wall that divided the bedroom and the bathroom. In complete darkness, I shut it off. Pretending I was blind. Which would I prefer? I thought about my body in bed doing nothing for the next seven hours. I kept score.

That night, the filmmaker wrote to say that he had thought of me. He wrote an email that said *thought of you* accompanied by a blue link. The link led to a scene in Antonioni's *L'Eclisse*—a film I still have not seen. In this scene, men in suits gesticulate on Milan's stock exchange floor—in this arena, the men are hysterical, shouting, flailing, buying, and selling, something I know little about. The sounds of their lusting slap through the Borsa. All that marble! I wondered why the filmmaker had thought of me. And then a buzzer goes off. The floor hushes. The death of a colleague is announced over a loud-speaker. One minute of silenzio for the dead man. Phones ring unanswered into the air. This silence is expensive. Not even the wealthiest man in the room can afford it. The buzzer sounds at one minute and the hysteria recommences, the clip cuts off. After, I read a transcript from a conversation between Antonioni, a self-described amateur painter, and Mark Rothko—Antonioni tells Rothko: *Your paintings are just like my films. About nothing. But with precision.*

Still unable to sleep, in bed with my computer, I moved, by hand, through the town of Eltingen—the birth town of Katherina Kepler. I wanted to find the statue erected in her honor. I made my way down Carl-Schmincke-Straße. On the map, I pressed the forward arrow and it took me unwillingly down a side street. I was lost straightaway.

The buildings are mainly framework houses and I was reminded of the photographs of Bernd and Hilla Becher. This region is apparently just north of the area heavily documented by the artist couple in the 1970s. The Bechers called the subjects of their photographs *anonymous sculptures*—absent of human figures: water towers, gas tanks, framework houses, furnaces, factories, coal bunkers. They no longer read as functional. Bernd once said they hoped to capture the structures in the way August Sander captured humans. Hilla once said that her aim, even as an apprentice photographer, had been to capture *silent objects*. She said that they photographed these things—the water towers, the furnaces—because they were honest and reflected what they did, that "a person always is who they want to be never who they are." And I thought, If something is silent is it honest?

I answered my own question as I moved much farther down Carl-Schmincke-Straße, past a facility where one can obtain a scuba license in a former church. There were no people out, just anonymous sculptures. The streets, the buildings, the parked cars, the signs—anonymous sculptures. There was no movement at all except for me along the arrow. Click, click, click. The arrow was heavy on the gas. I passed a red Peugeot at a red light. I thought, It will sit at that light forever! With another click, I wound up inside a car dealership, Autohaus Weember. Inside, a faceless man in a red tie walked toward me with white papers for a new vehicle. No, no, I was not there for a vehicle. I could not speak and he could not hear me. I turned and clicked the arrow and flipped around the room. I noticed I had left the door wide open behind me.

If there had been wind, it would have blown in just then. Cold, German wind. I thought, So this is what it's like to not even hear the sound of your own steps. A silent film with a score that is made with just the clanging landings and takeoffs of my thoughts. I was out of the dealership and back on the street. I had moved up and down this straße twice by then, so I decided to turn the next corner. Between a curtain store and a tanning salon, I found her there, Katherina Kepler made of stone the color of worn stone. She was the only human figure in town.

At her feet there was a small fountain. The water was a glowing and bright blue. Vacation blue. This blue did not reflect the sky. The sky in Eltingen looks like a blank sheet of paper. I felt suddenly like I had arrived somewhere empty-handed. I could imagine a ritual where young blond German football players line up and empty the contents of their lapis energy drinks at her feet. There is nothing lonelier than a monument, I decided as I looked at her. I moved in so close that I could no longer see her. Now she was a desert: empty, beige, a mass of grains that stretched to each edge of my screen and beyond. I moved up and down, up and down her whole body. Her face: sand drifts where a proverbial wind got too caught up with itself. I moved north to where her head met the sky, which appeared like the coast on a foggy day.

There was a small sign next to the fountain base: Werfen Sie keine Münzen—Do not toss coins. And below that another sign, the word *wünschend* with a red *X* running through it. I doubted Katherina wanted to be there, and I was sure she spent her days making wishes.

Outside it began to rain. I remembered the sound of rain hitting the air conditioner as I watched the rain hit the air conditioner. I moved down a narrow straße into a more residential part of town. With one click, there was snow powdered across the pavement. (It happened like this—with each click, the season, the weather, and the time of day was liable to shift.) The grass and the concrete and the tar roofs continued to prove their black existences just barely and I found myself in a cul-de-sac surrounded by the stone homes of upper-middle-class families. No longer framework homes but ones made of curved concrete—or was it stucco? Lights were on in these houses, and it was not difficult to picture what went on within: Insurance broker eats post-work Grützwurst as his preteen daughter performs a newly minted dance routine, when he notices, for the first time, the appearance of two small breasts. A tired financial officer of a large company known for the production of high-quality chocolate wrappers tells his wife that he has filed for bankruptcy but that they will be going on vacation to Busch Gardens, Tampa Bay, in a week's time—all expenses paid. With another click, I was in the driveway of a home at the far end of the circle, pushed flat against a silver Smart car with a Tankpool24 decal. With the next click, I was relocated to the foot of the driveway, where a small colony of recycling and garbage bins waited to be filled or emptied. In a space between the bins sat a pair of black boots and in the light snow I saw footsteps that led away from the boots and out of frame. With the next click, I arrived at the edge of the body of a man. Splayed on his back in the snow, barefoot.

One of the hazards of walking is witnessing. And I wondered, What is witnessing other than silence making an assertion? Right there, in front of me, was this new body to solve—and I felt that this *was* my body and that this rip inside of me had become perceivable.

This man was a man not a woman, on the older side too. And I was taken by his death position, which was an ironic and perfect simulation of Robert Walser's, who had also died in the snow—only 244 kilometers north, in Herisau. He too was splayed on his back, footsteps marching off frame. Death performed? I wondered. I moved in close to the snow on the soles of his pixelated feet. A cold body or a fresh body? I wondered. To the right of the man's head sat a golden bottle of San Benedetto Lemon Iced Tea.

Under the redundant German sky—a white drone, one held note—I thought of Celan's line from "Ashglory": "No one / witnesses for the / witness." And his phrase "Mundvoll Schweigen"—"mouthfuls of silence"—which made me think of eating snow, something I hadn't done for many years. Then, like a good little witness, I moved along.

I clicked away from the body and I clicked back down the road and thought about knocking on doors. Do you know this man? Showing the photograph I had taken. I imagined my always-tired super greeting me on the other side of each door—Can it wait till tomorrow? I clicked on; I was getting tired. I ended up out of the suburb and on the edge of the Black Forest in a band of mist. I decided to turn back because there was nothing to see. Celan, again, "In the Nothing—who stands there?" It was me— searching, in earnest, for the center of the fog.

The leak reprised, this time with a newfound passion. Again, I contacted the super—he was sorry but he was in Staten Island.

The following night I walked again, starting at the coordinates where I had drifted off, as though the walk were a book. The body in the snow was now thirty-plus kilometers south. I moved along the edge of the forest and arrived at an arrow that I was finally able to spin on. I could see houses the size of lozenges and low shifty hills—no snow. At first, in the forest, I was only seeing in separations of greens.

I was moving along just above the trees when I thought of a line from a TV documentary Herzog made about a woman, Juliane, the sole survivor of Peruvian LANSA Flight 508, which was struck by lightning in 1971, the day before Christmas. *I can still see the jungle beneath me, a deep green, like broccoli . . .* She said she thought this as she fell from the sky. Juliane had landed in the forest, still strapped into her seat, which had been the window seat. Her row had fallen as a unit. How could she have survived? She said that the updraft in the thundercloud had slowed her. As she dropped, she had a great spiral feeling. Like a falling maple seed (she saw herself as the seed, the rest of the row as the little wing). The air moving around her whole body. The fall was loud and then it was over. Silence is what escorts the fall into the state of having fallen. The tense of silence? Present, renewing itself always.

In an interview with an officer who led the search for the missing aircraft, the officer said that when the search team arrived at the site, they found that *the trees had been hung with the belongings of the travelers. Suitcases had opened in midair. Presents hung in the branches as if decorated with the fallen belongings. The trees stood as a funeral rite.*

I continued to move above the separations of greens. As I moved above what I still knew to be German trees, I felt the draft through the window touch the back of my neck like a cold, familiar hand. For eleven days, Juliane walked through the Amazon forest alone in search of anyone at all. She found a river, moved up it. Herzog—who was meant to be on the same flight, plans changed—was shooting his film based on a blond Spanish conquistador with big pink lips (Klaus Kinski) only a handful of miles away.

In the made-for-TV documentary, she and her husband, now a bat specialist and wasp specialist respectively, return with Herzog to the site of the crash to sift through the wreckage twenty years later: frame of a metal suitcase (still locked), heel of lady's shoe, hair curler, plastic tray (shortly before the plane crashed Juliane was served a sandwich). She was traveling with her mother, who was never found. On the day of the crash, all she could find were a Christmas cake, a baggie of candies, and three sets of legs coming out of the dirt concluding with feet, which she confirmed were not her mother's—eleven days later and near death, she came upon a small boat dragged up onto the sand. She poured gasoline from the fuel tank onto her wounds and collapsed. Her body was found alive by local fishermen. I smile now recalling the way Herzog says *toucan*.

As she was flown to the nearest hospital, she said, she recalled seeing herself down there. She recalled the sensation of seeing herself from above, walking up the river surrounded by uninterrupted green, the sensation of leaving herself behind.

At the end of this documentary, Herzog disclosed that he had invented all of her dreams as recounted in the film, and my thoughts on dreams were confirmed. I got up for a glass of water and carried myself back to bed—I scanned the forest, searching not for the wreckage, trees decorated with fallen belongings, but for a clearing in the trees, for a place to stop and sleep.

By March the left ear was worse off than the right. I had started eating a small amount of chocolate each night, Sno-Caps, which I kept in the fridge. Nothing I did seemed to make any difference. I began eating meat again too, steak. Caffeine. Gin if I felt like drinking, which I rarely did. Nothing seemed to make any difference. The weekly tests became monthly tests. Milligrams: up. Decibels, dollars, days: down. I went to see foreign movies for the subtitles and wore the carpenter's ear coverings from the hardware store. I kept score; I wrote it down.

The friend in Thessaloniki had not called for over a month; she was too in love with the anarchist now. The people from the trial recommended a signing school hosted at the building connected to a church in the neighborhood, the same place where people I knew attended Al-Anon meetings. I ignored the recommendation.

On the ides of March, I wrote to the girlfriend to recommend a play I thought she would like. I felt bad for not thanking her for letting me stay, but now too much time had passed—nearly seven weeks. She had started to frequent a dream I was having, which was unusual as I rarely remembered dreaming. In this new dream, the girlfriend appeared walking along a seaside road that I had driven off of into shallow water in a rented car, completely unscathed. Of course, I would not tell her about the dream.

I told her that the play was about a daughter of two gods who fell to Earth to bear witness to the general problems of people. The daughter of the gods was in a dissolving marriage. Like a tablet in water. She experienced terrible things—poverty, cruelty, and the routine of family life—and realized that human beings are to be pitied. Then she went back up to Heaven—*Everything can happen; everything is possible and likely* . . . I added that the play was referenced in a movie that takes place in an empty theater. In the movie, lingering after a rehearsal, the play's director enters into an honest and flirtatious conversation with his rising star, leading him to recall his affair with her late mother, another self-destructive actress. The girlfriend responded a day later. How was I? She wanted to know; she had been thinking of me. I told her I had developed a new habit of burning incense I'd been buying on Fourteenth Street—sandalwood, clove, cinnamon. She said that would give her a headache but that she would read the play, and she agreed that everything can happen; that everything is possible and likely. She asked if I was okay.

I still found myself returning to The Forum—now almost daily.

March 26, 4:55 p.m., Calgary1 shared a hyperlink to an article on Alan Shepard, the first American astronaut to go to space. Shepard was diagnosed with an affliction of the inner ear in 1964, grounding him after only one space flight. Years later, half-deaf, Shepard flew to the moon on the Apollo 14. Around the same time, the astronaut John Glenn slipped in his bathroom and damaged his inner ear and became bedridden. Glenn's and Shepard's vertigo led to brief widespread misconceptions about the hazards of flying in space.

Miss Baltic Sea was renovating. I had seen her in

the laundry room with an older man with kind eyes. I was happy for her. I kept making the tea I was not going to drink. I kept keeping score. I wrote down my 214th day in common milligrams. Hanne Darboven said her work made use of checks and sums but no one asked her what that meant because they were afraid to and then she died. She could have been a musician instead of an artist. But she said music could only be interpreted and she wanted to make something herself . . .

Then it was April Fool's Day and I was now approaching debt at the same rate I was approaching silence—steadily. I could see it like an island off the coast on a very clear day—sparkling, a silhouette, real. I could see it in the little black book, in the score. Now, it was seven months later and I sometimes woke up and had forgotten my own excuse. Every day was an excuse—sickness is leisure. I knew something would eventually change besides the milligrams and the sun. By mid-month, the girlfriend wrote almost daily because she had so many questions for me. Are you lonely?

I said that I still made many phone calls to feel not alone. That actually being out in the world felt too loud and overbearing now anyway. That being in the presence of things made me more aware of the way I was experiencing their absence—everything existed in silhouette. That being out at a restaurant made me feel more aware of what I was missing. That I could only handle one voice at a time, but that now I was good at reading lips. That I had been a happy person historically but that I was resistant to change. That I was someone who liked the things I liked just how they were, and that I even grieved the things I didn't like when they changed. That I was inconsolable on the final night of school plays because we would never pretend to be those characters, in that way, in that theater, in those hats, with that audience, at that time, ever again. One thing about silence was that once I reached it, I would finally have a constant. Something that would not go away. Now I thought of it as a goal, I told her, something to achieve, to arrive at like the top of a mountain or the center of a maze. But I said that I was also still holding out for recovery because there was an impossibility to my present that I would not accept so instead I was waiting. Drifting, she said. No, not drifting, I said, because there was no current. Okay, she said that I was treading then, not waiting, it was clear that my feet were not on any bottom, and I was not *wading* . . . She said treading is also a choice—unlike sinking. See, she said, I could still make decisions.

In May, I made the decision to sign up for signing school. In the first class, I met a thin man as we waited for the signing coach—it was a class for The Hearing. He said that he thanked God that his lessons were covered by insurance through his wife's job.

He said that his wife had successfully worked in advertising for many years. That she was depressed. Functionally so. He was a photographer who had not had a job for fifteen years. She made the money, he said. He was working on a seven-year project documenting the garden of an artist. The moment for children had come and gone. His wife had followed the advice of a therapist and in her midlife returned to school to follow her dreams. Her husband (he) was unaware she'd had dreams! She attended a program in museum conservation and excelled. She became an intern at a big museum in the moving-image department. The other intern was the age her daughter would be if she had had one. Her dead mother had told her life was about timing. Now she understood this, and not just on a conceptual level. The person she'd interned under died within six months, of ovarian cancer, and she was promoted to associate conservator of video art. She became increasingly satisfied by the shape of her days. But then, for some reason, he had become depressed. Clinically so. The garden he had been documenting each day for seven years no longer excited him at all. He'd realized it was just a garden.

So, on the weekends, they'd decided to do at least

one activity planned in advance as a couple. One weekend, they attended a Civil War reenactment in Green-Wood Cemetery, and his wife was deafened by the sound of a fake cannon fired off by an actor. She found herself depressed again. And the husband? He said he was actually very happy.

That day in the class we learned the signs for things around the kitchen: toaster, cupboard, microwave, dish towel, fruit bowl, clock, junk drawer. A young Frenchwoman in a pink shirt that said *You Owe Me* across the chest complained that there were several things she needed to learn before she learned the sign for *junk drawer.*

I knew spring had found its footing when the day trader returned, shouting about the rise and fall of numbers. His child was now old enough to scream at his mother. I left the window open all day again. By the end of May, the four-story tree right outside my window was removed just as life started to resuscitate on its branches. One morning, there was a compact man in the tree with a radio and spears on his boots that held him in the tree as he killed it very systematically. His radio played reggaeton and then a weather report in Spanish. From my window, I asked him if the tree was sick. The man said it was healthy. Too healthy! It was constricting the foundation of the building. He pointed to himself and said, La parca. In the news, the sonic attacks reappeared. A pair of scientists determined that the recording one diplomat had captured of the sound perfectly matched the mating song of the Indies short-tailed cricket. One expert noted that the cricket's song can be so persistent that you can hear them from inside a diesel truck going forty miles an hour on the highway . . . I added crickets to the list of things I feared.

It was a Friday night when my mother called again about the dying friend. It's time, she said, again like a prophet. When I arrived at the dying friend's home the next evening, the death-nurse offered me a soda. The sun was still up. It was bad timing—three ex-lovers all with hair the color of ash had just appeared as if delivered at once by God. Who would win her hand in death? One of them asked, Can I have a minute of your time? Imagine saying this to someone who is dying . . . He laid his hand on hers and she shooed it away like a wasp—with indignation as well as what looked like a hint of fear. I left. She died later that night. The following week, I lost male voices completely.

In the next signing lesson, we learned seasonally appropriate signs associated with the beach and camping—*tent, bug repellent, umbrella, low tide*. The Frenchwoman wore another statement tee; this one just said *fragile* in black stamp letters. She asked how to sign the word *disappointed*. Tip of dominant forefinger taps on the chin. The teacher said this could also be used for *disheartened*.

Then it was June in overdrive. When the city feels like the backcountry. I waited for the filmmaker to arrive. I had suggested we meet in the Village, near our old apartment, at one of the public benches with tables that have chessboards set into the concrete—a non-place. The community pool was in full swing on the other side of the silver fence. Three men hit a red ball against a white wall. It was all very simple and redemptive, the scene. Chlorine perfumed the air and there was a note of burning sugar from the bakery across the street. We were all baking alive. A group of young girls played Marco Polo. I had always wanted to swim in this pool as a kid but my mother had scared me about pink eye and Pontiac fever.

The filmmaker arrived with a long sandwich wrapped in wax paper. He was tanned. He had the look of a slack rope—waiting to be pulled in any direction. If I could live from scratch . . . he started to say. He asked if I could just let him speak even though I hadn't said anything. He asked if I was listening. I was listening and I told him I was listening. But when I sat across from him, I couldn't help but think only of myself.

Seeing him, I felt homesick for myself. As if I were

a place that could be returned to. I believed that I had such a hard time getting free of him because no one had known me the way he had, and so, I was convinced, I could never be known better. I feared that if I could not be known better, I could not be loved better. I had once seen myself and others as constants in a changing landscape, but now I could only see the inconsistencies. I am an only child, and people often asked, Are you two siblings? Though it was clear that we did not resemble each other at all. Maybe he had reflected back a part of me. I felt that he had become an external hard drive onto which a backup of my life had been saved, in increments, for good measure. I thought of what the landlord had said about always having two of the things you care about, like the favorite shirt. And I thought then that perhaps I cared too much about myself.

As he spoke, I was suddenly overwhelmed by what felt like the risk of forfeiting the external system that held otherwise-unrecoverable moments. I had the sense that I had outrun loss for a very, very long time.

He had said several things, strings of words that I had entirely missed but I didn't dare ask him to repeat. It was suddenly not that hot out anymore. He kept talking. He was very serious. He had come with questions. The game of Marco Polo had ended. He now appeared to me like a towel left out in summer rain.

When he finally paused just to catch his breath, I told him what I had avoided saying out loud, out of a fear that the action would reverse itself—I had just entered an unexpected remission.

I told him that it felt like a suspension of debt. That the silence itself had been traded like debt—its value increasing over time. He said to stop making analogies—but also that a remission is the cancellation of a debt and that I clearly didn't understand debt at all. He said I was always bad with money and that he would never share a bank account with me. Then he said, That was a joke. I said that I could still go deaf at any point, that the debt could come back. He said so can anything. He said, This news is unbelievable.

He said that the girlfriend had left him. I was listening. She had told him that chronology mattered and that it was clear now that I preceded her and always would. He asked if I thought that was true. I thought of the girlfriend and how beautiful she looked driving me from the airport with the wind all around her. He said something about two stars light-years away locked in a death dance—a union sure to end in collision and a possible supernova and meanwhile, both stars were unaware they were even "dancing." He said he would rather be a New York director anyway. He was moving back. He asked what I was doing for my birthday the next week.

He said we could organize something with all of our friends. I felt then that this conversation was like soaking. Penetration without pleasure, a delusional expectation of some great release. But then he pressed his mouth to mine—his God-given lips had been used many times to resuscitate a moment from fear and boredom, from pity and insecurity, from self-hatred and resentment, helplessness and confessions (to oneself) of having done harm. We wore down the minute. There was a forceful release—my engine kicking back . . . I knew there was no risk to calculate.

Eventually, it would start to rain but before that I had already decided to walk home, in tears.

Upstairs, the key seemed to be stuck in the door—as if I'd forced the wrong one into the lock—but it was the only key I had ever had and eventually it did open with force. Inside, I realized I hadn't eaten anything since that morning and felt faint from the heat. I thought I would walk to the Spanish restaurant around the corner with the napkins folded like pyramids, but when I went to leave, the knob just spun in an endless circle and the door would not open. I texted the super. He was in Staten Island. He said the screws were stripped. He asked if I had any tools.

I only had a hammer. I wanted to get out of this

situation on my own. I thought of what I could do: I could open the window, I could make a phone call, I could do anything, actually.

And then I realized the window was already open, all the way.

In July, I stopped keeping score. I wrote nothing down.

In August, one year after my first diagnosis, I traveled to Venice. The airline, as promised, honored my ticket. My mother, who rarely took off work, decided to join me. A celebration trip. She had only been to Venice once as a young child with her mother and sister just after her father died. A consolation trip.

We shared a bed in a small apartment that smelled of gasoline, operated by the owner of an adjacent hotel in the residential part of the Castello. The bedroom window looked out onto a defunct military marine base that was housing an off-site exhibition for the Venice Biennale. The entire show was visible from the window. The structure had been turned into a makeshift amphitheater by the artist representing Lithuania. The ring had been filled with true beach sand. On the sand, several actors performed a summer day on the shore with towels, watermelons, radios, magazines, dogs, beach umbrellas. There were children too, constructing mounds and moats.

Every other hour on the hour, the actors broke from their activities to perform a brief opera about tourism and climate change. The dogs barked during the soprano's aria. It's like a flash mob menagerie, I said to my mother. She told me she didn't know what a flash mob was. Minutes later, looking up from her phone, she asked me if I had known that in nineteenth-century Tasmania the term *flash mob* had been used to describe a subculture consisting of female prisoners. I had not. (Days later at checkout, we would receive a discount for the unexpected disruption, though we had not complained.)

As I unpacked, she undressed for a shower and looked out at the silent, still figures in the marina base.

Do you know the address here? You should always know the address of where you are, she said. I did not know. You should, she said. Did she? I asked. No.

And then she was naked. I discovered her pubic hair had gone gray.

She dressed again, went downstairs, and returned. There was no address. The stucco is just blank, she said.

On the morning of the first day, we visited the Scuola Grande di San Rocco, where we had to call the

Venezia Emergenza for a Swiss tourist, a man traveling alone, who had been knocked unconscious after
falling backward down a set of only three steps. The
church was full of tourists looking down at handheld
mirrors that a very short woman in a suit had supplied
at the entrance. The mirrors allowed the visitors to see
the ceiling, painted by Tintoretto, without having to
look up and strain their necks. The Swiss tourist had
been looking down at his mirror, reflecting *The Fall of
Manna in the Desert* or *Miracle of the Bronze Serpent*,
when he stepped off and hit his head on the landing
as we rounded a flight of stairs. Our proximity to the
calamity made us feel responsible for managing its
aftermath. There was no blood. The mirror had not
broken. The man was unresponsive. His camera remained around his neck. The small woman who had
supplied the mirrors shouted out first in Italian, then
in English, Hello! Does anyone know this man? Then
in six languages in addition to English:

Ciao! Qualcuno conosce quest'uomo?

Bonjour! Est-ce que quelqu'un connaît
cet homme?

¡Hola! ¿Conoces a este hombre?

誰かこの男の人知っていますか

Χαίρετε! Ξέρει κανείς αυτόν τον άνθρωπο.

Hallo! Kennst du diesen Mann?

The other tourists glanced up only briefly from their mirrors. As we waited for the Emergenza, they continued walking up to the main room. They had to step over his body in order to access the stairs. A woman who looked like Jane Fonda said, Pardon me, as she crossed over the man's chest. Finally, the responders took the man away by orange stretcher and we entered the chapel. We overheard a guide say it had once housed a small *Madonna with Child* by Giovanni Bellini (1481), which was stolen in 1993 and never recovered. The woman who looked like Jane Fonda was in fact Jane Fonda. She posed for a photograph with identical twins before the altar.

The girlfriend texted to recommend a belt shop on Calle de la Mandola. My mother wanted to visit a palazzo filled with textiles. I decided to skip the museum and spend an hour in the room before going to see Verdi's *Ernani*. I had not seen live music in over a year.

Back in the room, I got into the shower. The shampoo I'd bought from the pharmacy, Felce Azzurra, smelled like vanilla extract, and the conditioner like fresh laundry, masculine, treelike. Bright sun overtook the room even though it was after six. I sat in my towel on the bed and looked out at the military base: the ring, the sand, the several actors performing the summer day on the shore with towels, watermelons, radios, magazines, dogs. I told the girlfriend that I was back at the hotel and she texted saying when we first met she thought I did not like her. I said it took me time to become close to people but that once I was, I never lost touch. That I had never had a falling-out in my life. She said that was avoidance. I said I had gone to great lengths to spare the feelings of others at the expense of being truthful with myself. I put a white shirt on and sat in the chair by the window. I said I had a terrible fear of hurting people because I had decided from a young age that I was good. That no one had seen me do a bad thing. That I was innocent through and through . . .

I removed the white shirt I had just put on and then, in the chair with my arm outstretched above me, I looked up at myself there on the screen. I thought of tourists accidentally backing off cliffs and falling to their deaths while taking photos of themselves, in an attempt to prove that they were there, wherever they were. And then I thought of no consequences at all. I took my photo and sent it—proof of my innocence through and through . . .

And the girlfriend replied immediately and said that actually I was *very bad*. She sent a photo back, and I said she was worse. There wasn't anything to say beyond that. We stopped talking and instead we just sent images—image after image. We left words out of it.

Her hair was brown now—the same as mine, for another part. Paler than me, her skin fit her like a surgical glove. She was in a dark room. I could see only her. Our resemblance was more apparent now—for one moment I thought that the camera had not reversed. In Los Angeles it was after 2:00 a.m. She said, Can you do something for me?—I did. And I said, Can you show me something?—She did. She said, Can you show me something?—I did. And I said, Can you do something for me?—She did. And she said, Can you please? And I did. She asked if she could. And I said she had to wait. She said she had asked nicely. Ask again, I said. She said to call her so I could hear her. She said she cared about the order in which things happen and she said she wanted this to happen at the same time. And she said she couldn't wait anymore. I said she had to. And then I dialed and I thought there would be international charges. And then I was not listening. And then I could hear a siren go by in Los Angeles. And then she said, Good night, very quietly.

And sitting alone in the chair, I tried to connect this moment with another moment, this feeling with another feeling, but I had only myself in the chair. And with nothing to solve or defend, I felt very defenseless, which gave way to a very quick and heavy flood of embarrassment. And then, like the green ray, there was a bright flash of denial that couldn't sustain itself. *This* was what the doctor said to avoid. And then came a complete sadness that was very still and contained and twinkling, like water in a well. And this sadness felt in this moment like the greatest possible relief.

When my mother returned to change for dinner I was still naked and she said my cheeks looked flushed. I was still in the chair. She said the wet hair and wet towel would stain the chair's fabric. She said if I could see the people outside, they could see me. She said she had purchased the wrong tickets; we would be seeing the Vienna Boys' Choir and not an opera.

The next day, we walked through the Giardini along the Biennale pavilions, which were closed for an Italian holiday, but the park itself was open. An indecisive rain came down like spit and the puddles left over from the last night's flooding had turned into bodies of water that divided the cluster of buildings representing the different countries. It was just me and my mother between all of these confederations in shallow Italian mud. Switzerland was next to Venezuela and Russia looked out onto Germany;

Japan was a one-minute walk to Canada and Greece shared a Cyprus tree with Finland.

On our penultimate night, I watched my mother pack her bag. She sat on the ground before the great green curtain and the tall open window and rolled each article of clothing like a little bale of hay and spoke about how she wanted a little nap before dinner. She left out the things that she had planned to wear the following day, as well as on the airplane the morning after. She laid the items on the bed. Each item was either black or navy. Three pairs of black underwear. Two black button-downs. A blue sweater, a black sweater. A pair of blue linen pants, a pair of black polyester pants. Three black camisoles. And three sets of blue socks.

She looked very tired as she rested. Her face held the type of tiredness that one is unable to sleep off. I was the only child she had. I sat awake in the bed next to her and, with nothing to do for the next hour, I decided to walk again, beginning at the coordinates where I had left off. I was still in the woods, where it had to be summer. With the next click I was back in the snow on a road again with houses gated off from the road. I pressed forward and abruptly hit a brown wall. But when I pulled back I could see that I had actually collided with a small structure. It was a well that had a shingled roof covering it and a big silver bell suspended from a small rafter that hung over the stone enclosure of the well. At the edge was a small sign that read WÜNSCHE DIR ETWAS. It was a wishing well. Just by looking, I could hear a bell ringing long rings outward. My mother sat up abruptly. What is that? she said, as though the bell had woken her. She walked to the window.

Just outside the window, there was a thin man ringing a hand-held bell. I could hear the bell very clearly. He shouted, Arrotino! and we watched as a line of older women formed rapidly—each of them holding one or several large knives. He continued ringing the bell as the militia lined the canal. My mother returned to the bed and I stood and watched as the man sharpened the knives with his contraption. One by one, he greeted the women with two kisses.

The sun was going down and in an instant it seemed to force itself directly through the canal like a big foot into a small shoe. The sun made its way onto the knives and the knives reformed into blades of light. And as I thought about the synchronicity of the two bells—the ringing, the bell wringing itself out, I thought that silence is not dissimilar to a kitchen knife—something that catches the light, that cuts through, something that is necessary, something that dulls . . .

After the bells stopped, I could hear my mother snoring. Ringing with each breath her own little bell. It was very hot in the room and I switched on the white fan and pointed it toward her and I felt like God for this one second. For dinner I put on a red shirt, which is unlike me.

Later, I discovered the restaurant was entirely the same shade of red. And again I thought about the color-field painter who spoke about one patch of red being less red than a wall of red. We shared sardines with white polenta, bacalao with yellow polenta, mussels and clams with ginger steam, and fettuccini with monkfish. We sat without exchanging many words like two old lovers you witness, often while traveling. And by looking at the way the eyes of the lovers move around the room, it can be determined whether the silence between them is one of contentment or acceptance that something has run out. We discussed the dessert option and she had the courage to ask me, What are you working on?

•

On our final night, we found ourselves trapped in an unseasonable and severe flood. We learned this was the second-highest water surge in Venice on record since 1923. These surges have a name, the Acqua Alta. Before the flood, we took the Vaporetto from Arsenale to Santa Maria to eat dinner at a small restaurant that only served squid-ink pasta. Il Vuoto. It had been recommended by the friend who had gotten married—her father, a Venetian, had grown up with the father of the owner. (*Il vuoto* translates to "the void," a nod to the little, endless hole created on each plate by "the blackest pasta you will ever eat.")

The dining room, once full, rapidly emptied and we found ourselves alone in the restaurant with just the maître d', who was also the waiter, the runner, and the bartender. He leaned across the bar with a remote, rewinding a soccer play over and over again. The white dot spun across the screen, back to the foot of the player. In real time, the player had been running backward and now he ran forward to the ball. There was no music. As we paid the check, a group of two elderly German couples in expensive black clothing entered, very wet and gesticulating erratically. The host showed them to a table and promptly poured out four scotches.

When we exited the restaurant we found the small side street had flooded. The water came in over my boots. When we arrived at the first small bridge we found the tide had risen so high that boats could no longer pass through. As we approached the Grand Canal, the water continued to rise and the walkways were no longer distinguishable from the small canals. We held hands as we moved in a controlled panic through thigh-deep water that continued to rise. The dock for the Vaporetto had been submerged.

We walked along the edges of the buildings and followed blue signs with white arrows to San Marco. A man wearing a neon-orange vest walked with his spaniel, who swam alongside him.

All of San Marco was empty except for two people who stood at the opposite end of the square. The water was up to our hips and just the tops of the metal café chairs were visible. It was perfectly quiet. There was no wind or sound other than the lapping of water. The water filled the square and it all appeared very natural. It *was* natural. The moonlight went across the square like an open bay. Our panic had subsided. It was then that the sirens began to sound.

By morning the tide had receded. The only recorded death was of an elderly local man from Pellestrina, one of the many islands in the Venetian lagoon, who died when he was struck by lightning while using an electric water pump. I thought again of the line from *The Histories*: "When no cause can be discovered to events such as floods, droughts, frosts or even in politics, then the cause of these events may be fairly attributed to luck." But I realized it was not luck I was thinking of—I was thinking that if you think about something long enough, it will make sense even if you haven't made any sense of it at all—you've just gotten used to it. That sense is just acquainting yourself with nonsense over and over again. And I thought of the little black book

filled with the days, the doses, the decibels—the record, the nonsense.

When we had returned to the hotel the night before, we placed our shoes in the bathtub and I washed
my face as my mother picked up each shoe, drying
them one at a time with the Conair from under the
sink, which made the room smell of the lowest possible tide. After, we both got into the bed and she fell
asleep immediately. I was not tired at all.

From the dark room, I texted the filmmaker just
to say hello—with a photo of a bombolone, a photo
of the flooded San Marco, and a photo of two kids
pressing their faces and palms against the glass of a
water taxi's back window with tongues out—I said
that I hoped he was doing well, that I would be returning to the city tomorrow. But he had not replied
to any of my messages for over a month now. He was
treating me with silence. It is true, I thought, silence
is always replacing itself.

And I continued where I had left off . . .

I found myself walking again, in the height of
summer, down the center of a black road paved for
fast cars at the edge of the Appenzell town. When I
moved into the village, I could see there was a white
rectangular building, minimal and windowless with
a black clock and a golden rooster on top. It was
3:55 p.m. The cock glistened. And the light filled the
valley with rays that loved their lives as rays. And

the grass loved its life as grass. And the green loved its life as green. And houses accepted their lives as houses on the land, which seemed to rise and fall like a stomach in a perfect, easy sleep. And then I came upon a scene that sat like a painting that might catch you off guard and cause you to want to hold tightly on to something that you had already let go of. (Where did I put that? Why did I give it away?) There was a man with a rake in the grass. And three children next to a miniature red play car and another child crawling on hands and knees toward the light, toward a green mountain, and one bicycle lying on its side and a scooter standing up with a kickstand. And a red-and-yellow umbrella that looked like the ones making shade over the hot dog vendors in Central Park and Times Square. And I kept walking. It was still 3:55 p.m. By this point I knew I had taken off the layers I had started with because in the summer at 3:55 p.m. the sun is still laughing off its heat. And I thought that I had started this walk so many months ago, twelve of them, with so many sweaters on. That I was carrying all of these sweaters under my left arm in a great ball. And if I passed a sheep (where were all the sheep?), I might return the wool to the sheep. I felt I had just come upon myself walking there along this road and that I was now trying to get my attention. There were no animals, but I felt there were birds all around me, just out of sight.

They sang themselves to me, birds that I already had inside of my memory. Tropical birds, like in the recordings of the Amazon that had been played for me in elementary school. When you hear layers and layers of them you can hear the rain in their songs, small melodies bouncing off water. I felt then that the very surface of life appeared in a different light, a clearer and sharper light—that, like a tumbled rock, the silence had shellacked and buffed its surface. The black road unrolled itself. I wanted to say, Eliza, wait, stop there. Eliza! But I knew she could not hear me and I knew she would not be turning around, and I knew I had to let her walk where she was walking and that as soon as I let her out of my sight, I might not see her again.

ACKNOWLEDGMENTS

THANK YOU TO my agent, Harriet Moore, and to my editor, Kendall Storey, for your trust in this project and for the care, the clarity, the attention, and the life you have given it. Thank you to Kate Zambreno for saying, "This is a book," when it was a three-page essay, and for supporting this project at every turn and twist—it wouldn't exist without you. Thank you to Leslie Jamison for thinking with me and for helping me understand what I was thinking. Thank you to the doctors who looked at and listened so closely to me— Dr. Vambutas, Dr. Mazza, Dr. Stankovic, Dr. Nickerson, Dr. Dereberry, Dr. Scully, and Dr. Lustig. Thank you to Heather Ferguson, who hypnotized me once. Thank you to my parents, Dale and Michael, for your total love, which has made everything feel possible. Thank you to Jack Staffen for the beautiful salt-less meals, the life-music, the endless care, the grace, the listening, and so much more. Thank you to Angalis Field for the presentness, the most careful reading, the longest conversations, and for asking the questions no one else had. Thank you to Emmeline Clein, Tess Michelson, Stacey Streshinsky, and Hannah Gold for staying in this room with me. Thank you to Josie Hodson, Sophie Friedman Pappas, David Finnamore Rossler, Mick Kligler, Nawal Arjini, and Sally Rappaport. Thank you to Catherine Lippincott and Eliza Soros, and to Andrew Hale and Stephanie Simon. Thank you to Marty Skoble, Nancy Fales Garrett, and Ross Simonini, who have all taught me so much. Thank you to Josh Smith and Ross Simonini (again) for their beautiful conversation, which is referenced in the "gallery scene." Thank you to Dike Blair and to Canada Choate and Clemence White at Karma Gallery and to the Luiggi Ghirri Foundation and Matthew Marks Gallery. Thank you to William Basinski for *The Disintegration Loops*, which I listened to every day while editing. Thank you to *BOMB* magazine for first publishing what would later become a small section of this project. Thank you to Jim Hall, who will always be my neighbor. Thank you to the Atlantic Ocean, which I swam in a lot while writing this. And thank you to Keeper The Dog, who is so good at showing her love.

ELIZA BARRY CALLAHAN is a writer, artist, and musician from New York City. Her work has been published in *frieze*, *BOMB*, and *The Believer*. She received her MFA in writing from Columbia University. She was named a 2023 New York Foundation for the Arts fellow. *The Hearing Test* is her first novel.